**Series Volumes of
Haunted Library of Horror Classics:**

The Phantom of the Opera by Gaston Leroux (2020)

The Beetle by Richard Marsh (2020)

Vathek by William Beckford (2020)

The House on the Borderland
by William Hope Hodgson (2020)

The Parasite and Other Tales of Terror
by Arthur Conan Doyle (2021)

The King in Yellow by Robert W. Chambers (2021)

…and more forthcoming

D0961648

VATHEK

The Horror Writers Association
Haunted Library of Horror Classics
Presents:

VATHEK

Series Editors: Eric J. Guignard
and Leslie S. Klinger
With an introduction by Joe R. Lansdale

WILLIAM
BECKFORD

Poisoned Pen
PRESS

First published in 1786 as *An Arabian Tale, from an Unpublished Manuscript*
Copyright © 2020 by Horror Writers Association
Introduction © 2020 by Joe R. Lansdale
Additional supplemental material © 2020 by Eric J. Guignard and Leslie S. Klinger
Cover and internal design © 2020 by Sourcebooks
Cover design and illustration by Jeffrey Nguyen

Sourcebooks, Poisoned Pen Press, and the colophon
are registered trademarks of Sourcebooks.

All rights reserved. No part of this book may be reproduced in any form or by
any electronic or mechanical means including information storage and retrieval
systems—except in the case of brief quotations embodied in critical articles or
reviews—without permission in writing from its publisher, Sourcebooks.

Originally published as *Vathek* © William Beckford, 1816.
Translated from French by Samuel Henley.

The characters and events portrayed in this book are fictitious or
are used fictitiously. Any similarity to real persons, living or dead,
is purely coincidental and not intended by the author.

Published by Poisoned Pen Press, an imprint of Sourcebooks
P.O. Box 4410, Naperville, Illinois 60567-4410
(630) 961-3900
sourcebooks.com

Originally published as *An Arabian Tale, from an Unpublished Manuscript* in
1786. First published as *Vathek* in 1816. This edition issued based on the third
edition, revised and corrected, published in 1816 in England by W. Clarke.

Library of Congress Cataloging-in-Publication Data
Names: Beckford, William, author. | Lansdale, Joe R., writer of introduction.
Title: Vathek / William Beckford ; with an introduction by Joe R. Lansdale.
  Other titles: Vathek. English
Description: Naperville, IL : Poisoned Pen Press, [2020] | Series: Haunted
  library of horror classics | "Originally published as An Arabian Tale,
  from an unpublished manuscript in 1786. This edition is based on the
  third edition, revised and corrected, published as Vathek in 1816 in
  England by W. Clarke, London."
Identifiers: LCCN 2019059642 | (trade paperback)
Subjects: GSAFD: Gothic fiction. | Horror fiction.
Classification: LCC PQ1957.B29 V313 2020 | DDC 843/.5--dc23
LC record available at https://lccn.loc.gov/2019059642

Printed and bound in the United States of America.
SB 10 9 8 7 6 5 4 3 2 1

This edition of Vathek is presented by the Horror Writers Association, a nonprofit organization of writers and publishing professionals around the world, dedicated to promoting dark literature and the interests of those who write it. For more information on HWA, visit: horror.org.

CONTENTS

INTRODUCTION

Vathek is one peculiar novel, and so was its author, William Beckford. According to a recent edition of the book, his bio states he was born in 1759, son of an Alderman who was the Lord Mayor of London, twice.

In short, he was born into money. Enough money he was able to have a fine education, and was even taught music by Mozart, although I'm uncertain of the caliber of Beckford's musical skills.

He was well-traveled, well-educated, and perhaps totally decadent, accused of all manner of sexual debauchery with both women and men, and possibly young boys. He is noted for giving a lavish Christmas party where a dwarf answered the door, and food was in abundance and wine flowed as free as a downhill stream. The party is said to have taken place under an elaborate light show of some sort, and considering this occurred in the sixteenth century, the expense must have been enormous. It seems this elaborate party was one of the later influences for *Vathek*. For if there is one thing this short novel has is what that party had: Excess, a display of wealth, which in its strictest sense is representative of power, the obvious theme of *Vathek*.

Vathek is white-hot crazy, and considering, at least according to Beckford, it was written nonstop in French over three days and two nights, this is not surprising. It seems Beckford was trying to put a deep-sleep nightmare, or a waking dream, onto paper. A dream that feels like an episode from *The Arabian Nights* with a gothic nightmare inside of it.

The hero of *Vathek*, one Caliph Vathek, who has the evil eye, as well as some rather hedonistic desires, denounces Islam and, with assistance from his mother, sets out to obtain great supernatural powers and everlasting life. All of this, of course, involves a Satanic pact, as well as a travelogue of dark exploration, culminating in what might be described as an examination of the lower regions of Hell.

From one bizarre moment to the next, this novel taps into all those little hidden areas that our personalities guard or fear. It allows us to tour places most of us wouldn't want to go, but don't mind seeing through a kind of literary glass, like visiting an aquarium and observing a shark enjoy chunks of bleeding meat at mealtime.

Vathek can be rambling, uncertain of intent, and it has moments when its author seems to be overcome by the pure energy of the writing. It is humorous for a while, then less so, and finally so strange it nears running off the rails and tumbling into an abyss. But there is seldom a moment when it isn't compelling. Even its failures are grand and stimulating, like watching a boxer who is knocked down repeatedly, continue to rise from the mat and keep on swinging.

To suggest this novel has not aged would be disingenuous, for it has, both in style and in social mores. In fact, its impact on earlier writers and their works outweighs the actual weight of the novel for the casual modern reader, but this steamy window into a historically important exercise in writing mania is significant to the fields of gothic and horror writing, as well as what was once referred to as Orientalism.

There is absolutely nothing like it.

Joe R. Lansdale
April 7, 2019
Nacogdoches, Texas

VATHEK

VATHEK, ninth Caliph[1] of the race of the Abassides, was the son of Motassem, and the grandson of Haroun al Raschid. From an early accession to the throne, and the talents he possessed to adorn it, his subjects were induced to expect that his reign would be long and happy. His figure was pleasing and majestic; but when he was angry, one of his eyes became so terrible[2], that no person could bear to behold it; and the wretch upon whom it was fixed, instantly fell backward, and sometimes expired. For fear, however, of depopulating his dominions and making his palace desolate, he but rarely gave way to his anger.

Being much addicted to women and the pleasures of the table, he sought by his affability, to procure agreeable companions; and he succeeded the better as his generosity was unbounded and his indulgencies unrestrained: for he did not think, with the Caliph Omar Ben Abdalaziz[3] that it was necessary to make a hell of this world to enjoy paradise in the next.

He surpassed in magnificence all his predecessors. The palace of Alkoremi, which his father, Motassem, had erected on the hill of Pied Horses, and which commanded the whole city of Samarah[4], was, in his idea far too scanty: he added, therefore, five wings, or rather other palaces, which he destined for the particular gratification of each of the senses.

In the first of these were tables continually covered with the most exquisite dainties; which were supplied both by night and by day, according to their constant consumption; whilst the most delicious wines and the choicest cordials flowed forth from a hundred fountains that were never exhausted. This palace was called *The Eternal or Unsatiating Banquet.*

The second was styled, *The Temple of Melody,* or *The Nectar of the Soul.* It was inhabited by the most skilful musicians and admired poets of the time; who not only displayed their talents within, but dispersing in bands without, caused every surrounding scene to reverberate their songs; which were continually varied in the most delightful succession[5].

The palace named *The Delight of the Eyes,* or *The Support of Memory,* was one entire enchantment. Rarities, collected from every corner of the earth were there found in such profusion as to dazzle and confound, but for the order in which they were arranged. One gallery exhibited the pictures of the celebrated Mani[6], and statues, that seemed to be alive. Here a well-managed perspective attracted the sight; there the magic of optics agreeably deceived it: whilst the naturalist on his part, exhibited in their several classes the various gifts that Heaven had bestowed on our globe. In a word, Vathek omitted nothing in this palace, that might gratify the curiosity of those who resorted to it, although he was not able to satisfy his own; for, of all men, he was the most curious.

The Palace of Perfumes, which was termed likewise *The Incentive to Pleasure,* consisted of various halls, where the different perfumes which the earth produces were kept perpetually burning in censers of gold. Flambeaux and aromatic lamps were here lighted in open day. But the too powerful effects of this agreeable delirium might be alleviated by descending into an immense garden, where an assemblage of every fragrant flower diffused through the air the purest odours.

The fifth palace, denominated *The Retreat of Mirth, or the Dangerous*, was frequented by troops of young females beautiful as the Houris[7], and not less seducing; who never failed to receive with caresses, all whom the Caliph allowed to approach them, and enjoy a few hours of their company.

Notwithstanding the sensuality in which Vathek indulged, he experienced no abatement in the love of his people, who thought that a sovereign giving himself up to pleasure, was as able to govern, as one who declared himself an enemy to it. But the unquiet and impetuous disposition of the Caliph would not allow him to rest there. He had studied so much for his amusement in the life-time of his father, as to acquire a great deal of knowledge, though not a sufficiency to satisfy himself; for he wished to know every thing; even sciences that did not exist. He was fond of engaging in disputes with the learned, but did not allow them to push their opposition with warmth. He stopped with presents the mouths of those whose mouths could be stopped; whilst others, whom his liberality was unable to subdue, he sent to prison to cool their blood; a remedy that often succeeded.

Vathek discovered also a predilection for theological controversy; but it was not with the orthodox that he usually held. By this means he induced the zealots to oppose him, and then persecuted them in return; for he resolved, at any rate, to have reason on his side.

The great prophet, Mahomet, whose vicars the caliphs are, beheld with indignation from his abode in the seventh heaven[8], the irreligious conduct of such a vicegerent. "Let us leave him to himself," said he to the Genii[9], who are always ready to receive his commands: "let us see to what lengths his folly and impiety will carry him: if he run into excess, we shall know how to chastise him. Assist him, therefore, to complete the tower[10], which, in imitation of Nimrod, he hath begun; not, like that great warrior, to escape being drowned, but from the insolent curiosity of penetrating the secrets of heaven:—he will not divine the fate that awaits him."

The Genii obeyed; and, when the workmen had raised their structure a cubit* in the day time, two cubits more were added in the night. The expedition, with which the fabric arose, was not a little flattering to the vanity of Vathek: he fancied, that even insensible matter shewed a forwardness to subserve his designs; not considering, that the successes of the foolish and wicked form the first rod of their chastisement.

His pride arrived at its height, when having ascended, for the first time, the fifteen hundred stairs of his tower, he cast his eyes below, and beheld men not larger than pismires;† mountains, than shells; and cities, than bee-hives. The idea, which such an elevation inspired of his own grandeur, completely bewildered him: he was almost ready to adore himself; till, lifting his eyes upward, he saw the stars as high above him as they appeared when he stood on the surface of the earth. He consoled himself, however, for this intruding and unwelcome perception of his littleness, with the thought of being great in the eyes of others; and flattered himself that the light of his mind would extend beyond the reach of his sight, and extort from the stars the decrees of his destiny.

With this view, the inquisitive Prince passed most of his nights on the summit of his tower, till becoming an adept in

---

*A "cubit" is an ancient unit of measurement, the length of a man's forearm, about eighteen inches or forty-four centimeters.
†Ants.

the mysteries of astrology, he imagined that the planets had disclosed to him the most marvellous adventures, which were to
be accomplished by an extraordinary personage, from a country altogether unknown. Prompted by motives of curiosity, he
had always been courteous to strangers; but, from this instant,
he redoubled his attention, and ordered it to be announced, by
sound of trumpet through all the streets of Samarah, that no one
of his subjects, on peril of his displeasure, should either lodge or
detain a traveller, but forthwith bring him to the palace.

Not long after this proclamation, arrived in his metropolis a
man so abominably hideous that the very guards, who arrested
him, were forced to shut their eyes, as they led him along: the
Caliph himself appeared startled at so horrible a visage; but
joy succeeded to this emotion of terror, when the stranger displayed to his view such rarities[11] as he had never before seen,
and of which he had no conception.

In reality, nothing was ever so extraordinary as the merchan-
dize this stranger produced: most of his curiosities, which were
not less admirable for their workmanship than splendour, had,
besides, their several virtues described on a parchment fastened
to each. There were slippers, which, by spontaneous springs,
enabled the feet to walk; knives, that cut without motion of the
hand; sabres, that dealt the blow at the person they were wished
to strike; and the whole enriched with gems, that were hitherto
unknown.

The sabres, especially, the blades of which, emitted a dazzling
radiance, fixed, more than all the rest, the Caliph's attention;
who promised himself to decipher, at his leisure, the uncouth
characters engraven on their sides. Without, therefore, demanding their price, he ordered all the coined gold to be brought from
his treasury, and commanded the merchant to take what he
pleased. The stranger obeyed, took little, and remained silent.

Vathek, imagining that the merchant's taciturnity was occa-sioned by the awe which his presence inspired, encouraged him to advance; and asked him, with an air of condescension, who he was? whence he came? and where he obtained such beautiful commodities? The man, or rather monster, instead of making a reply, thrice rubbed his forehead, which, as well as his body, was blacker than ebony; four times clapped his paunch, the projec-tion of which was enormous; opened wide his huge eyes, which glowed like firebrands; began to laugh with a hideous noise, and discovered his long amber-coloured teeth, bestreaked with green.

The Caliph, though a little startled, renewed his inquiries, but without being able to procure a reply. At which, beginning to be ruffled, he exclaimed:—"Knowest thou, wretch, who I am, and at whom thou art aiming thy gibes?"—Then, address-ing his guards, "Have ye heard him speak? is he dumb?"—"He hath spoken," they replied, "but to no purpose." "Let him speak then again," said Vathek, "and tell me who he is, from whence he came, and where he procured these singular curiosities; or I swear, by the ass of Balaam,* that I will make him rue his pertinacity."

This menace was accompanied by one of the Caliph's angry and perilous glances, which the stranger sustained without the slightest emotion; although his eyes were fixed on the terrible eye of the Prince.

No words can describe the amazement of the courtiers, when they beheld this rude merchant withstand the encounter unshocked. They all fell prostrate with their faces on the ground, to avoid the risk of their lives; and would have continued in the

---

*In Numbers, Balaam, a diviner, is prevented from consorting with the princes of Moab by the actions of his ass, who speaks with him and reveals the hand of God causing the ass's actions.

same abject posture, had not the Caliph exclaimed in a furious tone—"Up, cowards! seize the miscreant! see that he be committed to prison, and guarded by the best of my soldiers! Let him, however, retain the money I gave him; it is not my intent to take from him his property; I only want him to speak."

No sooner had he uttered these words, than the stranger was surrounded, pinioned and bound with strong fetters, and hurried away to the prison of the great tower; which was encompassed by seven empalements of iron bars, and armed with spikes in every direction, longer and sharper than spits. The Caliph, nevertheless, remained in the most violent agitation. He sat down indeed to eat; but, of the three hundred dishes that were daily placed before him, he could taste of no more than thirty-two.

A diet, to which he had been so little accustomed, was sufficient of itself to prevent him from sleeping; what then must be its effect when joined to the anxiety that preyed upon his spirits? At the first glimpse of dawn he hastened to the prison, again to importune this intractable stranger; but the rage of Vathek exceeded all bouuds on finding the prison empty; the grates burst asunder, and his guards lying lifeless around him. In the paroxism of his passion he fell furiously on the poor carcasses, and kicked them till evening without intermission. His courtiers and vizirs exerted their efforts to soothe his extravagance; but, finding every expedient ineffectual, they all united in one vociferation—"The Caliph is gone mad! the Caliph is out of his senses!"

This outcry, which soon resounded through the streets of Samarah, at length reached the ears of Carathis, his mother, who flew in the utmost consternation to try her ascendancy on the mind of her son. Her tears and caresses called off his attention; and he was prevailed upon, by her intreaties, to be brought back to the palace.

Carathis, apprehensive of leaving Vathek to himself, had him put to bed; and, seating herself by him, endeavoured by her conversation to appease and compose him. Nor could any one have attempted it with better success; for the Caliph not only loved her as a mother, but respected her as a person of superior genius. It was she who had induced him, being a Greek herself, to adopt the sciences and systems of her country which all good Mussulmans hold in such thorough abhorrence.

Judiciary astrology was one of those sciences, in which Carathis was a perfect adept. She began, therefore, with remind-ing her son of the promise which the stars had made him; and intimated an intention of consulting them again. "Alas!" said the Caliph as soon as he could speak, "what a fool I have been! not for having bestowed forty thousand kicks on my guards, who so tamely submitted to death; but for never considering that this extraordinary man was the same that the planets had foretold; whom, instead of ill-treating, I should have conciliated by all the arts of persuasion."

"The past," said Carathis, "cannot be recalled; but it behoves us to think of the future: perhaps, you may again see the object you so much regret: it is possible the inscriptions on the sabres will afford information. Eat, therefore, and take thy repose, my dear son. We will consider, to-morrow, in what manner to act."

Vathek yielded to her counsel as well as he could, and arose in the morning with a mind more at ease. The sabres he com-manded to be instantly brought; and, poring upon them, through a coloured glass, that their glittering might not dazzle, he set himself in earnest to decipher the inscriptions; but his reiterated attempts were all of them nugatory: in vain did he beat his head, and bite his nails; not a letter of the whole was he able to ascertain. So unlucky a disappointment would have undone him again, had not Carathis, by good fortune, entered the apartment.

"Have patience, my son!" said she:—"you certainly are possessed of every important science; but the knowledge of languages is a trifle at best; and the accomplishment of none but a pedant. Issue a proclamation, that you will confer such rewards as become your greatness, upon any one that shall interpret what you do not understand, and what is beneath you to learn; you will soon find your curiosity gratified."

"That may be," said the Caliph; "but, in the mean time, I shall be horribly disgusted by a crowd of smatterers, who will come to the trial as much for the pleasure of retailing their jargon, as from the hope of gaining the reward. To avoid this evil, it will be proper to add, that I will put every candidate to death, who shall fail to give satisfaction: for, thank Heaven! I have skill enough to distinguish, whether one translates or invents."

"Of that I have no doubt," replied Carathis; "but, to put the ignorant to death is somewhat severe, and may be productive of dangerous effects. Content yourself with commanding their beards to be burnt:[12]—beards in a state, are not quite so essential as men."

The Caliph submitted to the reasons of his mother; and, sending for Morakanabad, his prime vizir, said,—"Let the common criers proclaim, not only in Samarah, but throughout every city in my empire, that whosoever will repair hither and decipher certain characters which appear to be inexplicable, shall experience that liberality for which I am renowned; but, that all who fail upon trial shall have their beards burnt off to the last hair. Let them add, also, that I will bestow fifty beautiful slaves, and as many jars of apricots from the Isle of Kirmith, upon any man that shall bring me intelligence of the stranger."

The subjects of the Caliph, like their sovereign, being great admirers of women and apricots from Kirmith, felt their mouths water at these promises, but were totally unable to gratify their hankering; for no one knew what had become of the stranger.

As to the Caliph's other requisition, the result was different. The learned, the half learned, and those who were neither, but fancied themselves equal to both, came boldly to hazard their beards, and all shamefully lost them. The exaction of these forfeitures, which found sufficient employment for the eunuchs, gave them such a smell of singed hair, as greatly to disgust the ladies of the seraglio, and to make it necessary that this new occupation of their guardians should be transferred to other hands.

At length, however, an old man presented himself, whose beard was a cubit and a half longer than any that had appeared before him. The officers of the palace whispered to each other, as they ushered him in—"What a pity, oh! what a great pity that such a beard should be burnt!" even the Caliph, when he saw it, concurred with them in opinion; but his concern was entirely needless. This venerable personage read the characters with facility, and explained them verbatim as follows: "We were made where every thing is well made: we are the least of the wonders of a place where all is wonderful and deserving, the sight of the first potentate on earth."

"You translate admirably!" cried Vathek; "I know to what these marvellous characters allude. Let him receive as many robes of honour and thousands of sequins of gold as he hath spoken words. I am in some measure relieved from the perplexity that embarrassed me!" Vathek invited the old man to dine, and even to remain some days in the palace.

Unluckily for him, he accepted the offer; for the Caliph having ordered him next morning to be called, said—"Read again to me what you have read already; I cannot hear too often the promise that is made me—the completion of which I languish to obtain." The old man forthwith put on his green spectacles, but they instantly dropped from his nose, on perceiving that the characters he had read the day preceding, had given place to others of different import. "What ails you?" asked the Caliph; "and why these symptoms of wonder?"—"Sovereign of the world!" replied the old man, "these sabres hold another language today from that they yesterday held."—"How say you?" returned Vathek:—"but it matters not; tell me, if you can, what they mean."—"It is this, my lord," rejoined the old man: "Woe to the rash mortal who seeks to know that of which he should remain ignorant; and to undertake that which surpasseth his power!"—"And woe to thee!" cried the Caliph, in a burst of indignation, "to-day thou art void of understanding: begone from my presence, they shall burn but the half of thy beard, because thou wert yesterday fortunate in guessing:—my gifts I never resume." The old man, wise enough to perceive he had luckily escaped, considering the folly of disclosing so disgusting a truth, immediately withdrew and appeared not again.

But it was not long before Vathek discovered abundant reason to regret his precipitation; for, though he could not decipher the characters himself, yet, by constantly poring upon them, he plainly perceived that they every day changed; and, unfortunately, no other candidate offered to explain them. This perplexing occupation inflamed his blood, dazzled his sight, and brought on such a giddiness and debility that he could hardly support himself. He failed not, however, though in so reduced a condition, to be often carried to his tower, as he flattered himself that he might there read in the stars, which he went to consult, something more congruous to his wishes; but in this his hopes were deluded: for his eyes, dimmed by the vapours of his head, began to subserve his curiosity so ill, that he beheld nothing but a thick, dun cloud, which he took for the most direful of omens.

Agitated with so much anxiety, Vathek entirely lost all firm-ness; a fever seized him, and his appetite failed. Instead of being one of the greatest eaters, he became as distinguished for drink-ing. So insatiable was the thirst which tormented him, that his mouth, like a funnel, was always open to receive the various liquors that might be poured into it, and especially cold water, which calmed him more than any other.

This unhappy prince, being thus incapacitated for the enjoy-ment of any pleasure, commanded the palaces of the five senses to be shut up; forebore to appear in public, either to display his magnificence, or administer justice, and retired to the inmost apartment of his harem. As he had ever been an excellent husband, his wives, overwhelmed with grief at his deplorable situation, incessantly supplied him with prayers for his health, and water for his thirst.

In the mean time the Princess Carathis, whose affliction no words can describe, instead of confining herself to sobbing and tears, was closetted daily with the vizir Morakanabad, to find out some cure, or mitigation, of the Caliph's disease. Under the persuasion that it was caused by enchantment, they turned over together, leaf by leaf, all the books of magic that might point out a remedy; and caused the horrible stranger, whom they accused as the enchanter, to be every where sought for, with the strictest diligence.

At the distance of a few miles from Samarah stood a high mountain, whose sides were swarded with wild thyme and basil, and its summit overspread with so delightful a plain, that it might have been taken for the Paradise destined for the faithful. Upon it grew a hundred thickets of eglantine and other fragrant shrubs; a hundred arbours of roses, entwined with jessamine and honey-suckle; as many clumps of orange trees, cedar, and citron; whose branches, interwoven with the palm, the pomegranate, and the vine, presented every luxury that could regale the eye or the taste. The ground was strewed with violets, hare-bells, and pansies; in the midst of which numerous tufts of jonquils, hyacinths, and carnations perfumed the air. Four fountains, not less clear than deep, and so abundant as to slake the thirst of ten armies, seemed purposely placed here, to make the scene more resemble the garden of Eden watered by four sacred rivers. Here, the nightingale sang the birth of the rose, her well-beloved, and, at the same time, lamented its short-lived beauty; whilst the dove deplored the loss of more substantial pleasures; and the wakeful lark hailed the rising light that re-animates the whole creation. Here, more than any where, the mingled melodies of birds expressed the various passions which inspired them; and the exquisite fruits, which they pecked at pleasure, seemed to have given them a double energy.

To this mountain Vathek was sometimes brought, for the sake of breathing a purer air; and, especially, to drink at will of the four fountains. His attendants were his mother, his wives, and some eunuchs, who assiduously employed themselves in filling capacious bowls of rock crystal, and emulously presenting them to him. But it frequently happened, that his avidity exceeded their zeal, insomuch, that he would prostrate himself upon the ground to lap the water, of which he could never have enough.

One day, when this unhappy Prince had been long lying in so debasing a posture, a voice, hoarse but strong, thus addressed him: "Why dost thou assimilate thyself to a dog, O Caliph, proud as thou art of thy dignity and power?" At this apostrophe, he raised up his head, and beheld the stranger that had caused him so much affliction. Inflamed with anger at the sight, he exclaimed:—"Accursed Giaour[13]! what comest thou hither to do?—is it not enough to have transformed a prince, remarkable for his agility, into a water budget? Perceivest thou not, that I may perish by drinking to excess, as well as by thirst?"

"Drink then this draught," said the stranger, as he presented to him a phial of a red and yellow mixture: "and, to satiate the thirst of thy soul, as well as of thy body, know, that I am an Indian; but, from a region of India, which is wholly unknown."

The Caliph, delighted to see his desires accomplished in part, and flattering himself with the hope of obtaining their entire fulfilment, without a moment's hesitation swallowed the potion, and instantaneously found his health restored, his thirst appeased, and his limbs as agile as ever. In the transports of his joy, Vathek leaped upon the neck of the frightful Indian, and kissed his horrid mouth and hollow cheeks, as though they had been the coral lips and the lilies and roses of his most beautiful wives.

Nor would these transports have ceased, had not the eloquence of Carathis repressed them. Having prevailed upon him to return to Samarah, she caused a herald to proclaim as loudly as possible—"The wonderful stranger hath appeared again; he hath healed the Caliph;—he hath spoken! he hath spoken!"

Forthwith, all the inhabitants of this vast city quitted their habitations, and ran together in crowds to see the procession of Vathek and the Indian, whom they now blessed as much as they had before execrated, incessantly shouting—"He hath healed our sovereign;—he hath spoken! he hath spoken!" Nor were these words forgotten in the public festivals, which were celebrated the same evening, to testify the general joy; for the poets applied them as a chorus to all the songs they composed on this interesting subject.

The Caliph, in the meanwhile, caused the palaces of the senses to be again set open; and, as he found himself naturally prompted to visit that of Taste in preference to the rest, immediately ordered a splendid entertainment, to which his great officers and favourite courtiers were all invited. The Indian, who was placed near the Prince, seemed to think that, as a proper acknowledgment of so distinguished a privilege, he could neither eat, drink, nor talk too much. The various dainties were no sooner served up than they vanished, to the great mortification of Vathek, who piqued himself on being the greatest eater alive; and, at this time in particular, was blessed with an excellent appetite.

The rest of the company looked round at each other in amazement; but the Indian, without appearing to observe it, quaffed large bumpers to the health of each of them; sung in a style altogether extravagant; related stories, at which he laughed immoderately; and poured forth extemporaneous verses, which would not have been thought bad, but for the strange grimaces with which they were uttered. In a word, his loquacity was equal to that of a hundred astrologers; he ate as much as a hundred porters, and caroused in proportion.

The Caliph, notwithstanding the table had been thirty-two times covered, found himself incommoded by the voraciousness of his guest, who was now considerably declined in the Prince's esteem. Vathek, however, being unwilling to betray the chagrin he could hardly disguise, said in a whisper to Bababalouk, the chief of his eunuchs, "You see how enormous his performances are in every way; what would be the consequence should he get at my wives!—Go! redouble your vigilance, and be sure look well to my Circassians, who would be more to his taste than all of the rest."

The bird of the morning had thrice renewed his song, when the hour of the Divan[14] was announced. Vathek, in gratitude to his subjects, having promised to attend, immediately arose from table, and repaired thither, leaning upon his vizir who could scarcely support him: so disordered was the poor Prince by the wine he had drunk, and still more by the extravagant vagaries of his boisterous guest.

The viziers, the officers of the crown and of the law, arranged themselves in a semicircle about their sovereign, and preserved a respectful silence; whilst the Indian, who looked as cool as if he had been fasting, sat down without ceremony on one of the steps of the throne, laughing in his sleeve at the indignation with which his temerity had filled the spectators.

The Caliph, however, whose ideas were confused, and whose head was embarrassed, went on administering justice at haphazard; till at length the prime vizir[15], perceiving his situation, hit upon a sudden expedient to interrupt the audience and rescue the honour of his master, to whom he said in a whisper:—"My lord, the Princess Carathis, who hath passed the night in consulting the planets, informs you, that they portend you evil, and the danger is urgent. Beware, lest this stranger, whom you have so lavishly recompensed for his magical gewgaws, should make some attempt on your life: his liquor, which at first had the appearance of effecting your cure, may be no more than a poison, the operation of which will be sudden.—Slight not this surmise: ask him, at least, of what it was compounded, whence he procured it; and mention the sabres, which you seem to have forgotten."

Vathek, to whom the insolent airs of the stranger became every moment less supportable, intimated to his vizir, by a wink of acquiescence, that he would adopt his advice; and, at once turning towards the Indian, said—"Get up, and declare in full Divan of what drugs was compounded the liquor you enjoined me to take, for it is suspected to be poison: give also, that explanation I have so earnestly desired, concerning the sabres you sold me, and thus shew your gratitude for the favours heaped on you."

Having pronounced these words, in as moderate a tone as he well could, he waited in silent expectation for an answer. But the Indian, still keeping his seat, began to renew his loud shouts of laughter, and exhibit the same horrid grimaces he had shewn them before, without vouchsafing a word in reply. Vathek, no longer able to brook such insolence, immediately kicked him from the steps; instantly descending, repeated his blow; and persisted, with such assiduity, as incited all who were present to follow his example. Every foot was up and aimed at the Indian, and no sooner had any one given him a kick, than he felt himself constrained to reiterate the stroke.

The stranger afforded them no small entertainment: for, being both short and plump, he collected himself into a ball, and rolled round on all sides, at the blows of his assailants, who pressed after him, wherever he turned, with an eagerness beyond conception, whilst their numbers were every moment increasing. The ball indeed, in passing from one apartment to another, drew every person after it that came in its way; insomuch, that the whole palace was thrown into confusion and resounded with a tremendous clamour. The women of the harem, amazed at the uproar, flew to their blinds to discover the cause; but, no sooner did they catch a glimpse of the ball, than, feeling themselves unable to refrain, they broke from the clutches of their eunuchs, who, to stop their flight, pinched them till they bled; but, in vain: whilst themselves, though trembling with terror at the escape of their charge, were as incapable of resisting the attraction.

After having traversed the halls, galleries, chambers, kitchens, gardens, and stables of the palace, the Indian at last took his course through the courts; whilst the Caliph, pursuing him closer than the rest, bestowed as many kicks as he possibly could; yet, not without receiving now and then a few which his competitors, in their eagerness, designed for the ball.

Carathis, Morakanabad, and two or three old vizirs, whose wisdom had hitherto withstood the attraction, wishing to prevent Vathek from exposing himself in the presence of his subjects, fell down in his way to impede the pursuit: but he, regardless of their obstruction, leaped over their heads, and went on as before. They then ordered the Muezins[16] to call the people to prayers; both for the sake of getting them out of the way, and of endeavouring, by their petitions, to avert the calamity; but neither of these expedients was a whit more successful. The sight of this fatal ball was alone sufficient to draw after it every beholder. The Muezins themselves, though they saw it but at a distance, hastened down from their minarets, and mixed with the crowd; which continued to increase in so surprising a manner, that scarce an inhabitant was left in Samarah, except the aged; the sick, confined to their beds; and infants at the breast, whose nurses could run more nimbly without them. Even Carathis, Morakanabad, and the rest, were all become of the party. The shrill screams of the females, who had broken from their apartments, and were unable to extricate themselves from the pressure of the crowd, together with those of the eunuchs jostling after them, and terrified lest their charge should escape from their sight; the execrations of husbands, urging forward and menacing each other; kicks given and received; stumblings and overthrows at every step; in a word, the confusion that universally prevailed, rendered Samarah like a city taken by storm, and devoted to absolute plunder. At last, the cursed Indian, who still preserved his rotundity of figure, after passing through all the streets and public places, and leaving them empty, rolled onwards to the plain of Catoul, and entered the valley at the foot of the mountain of the four fountains.

As a continual fall of water had excavated an immense gulph in the valley whose opposite side was closed in by a steep acclivity, the Caliph and his attendants were apprehensive, lest the ball should bound into the chasm, and, to prevent it, redoubled their efforts, but in vain. The Indian persevered in his onward direction; and, as had been apprehended, glancing from the precipice with the rapidity of lightning, was lost in the gulph below.

Vathek would have followed the perfidious Giaour, had not an invisible agency arrested his progress. The multitude that pressed after him were at once checked in the same manner, and a calm instantaneously ensued. They all gazed at each other with an air of astonishment, and notwithstanding that the loss of veils and turbans, together with torn habits, and dust blended with sweat, presented a most laughable spectacle, yet there was not one smile to be seen. On the contrary, all with looks of confusion and sadness returned in silence to Samarah, and retired to their inmost apartments, without ever reflecting, that they had been impelled by an invisible power into the extravagance, for which they reproached themselves: for it is but just that men, who so often arrogate to their own merit the good of which they are but instruments, should also attribute to themselves absurdities which they could not prevent.

The Caliph was the only person who refused to leave the valley. He commanded his tents to be pitched there, and stationed himself on the very edge of the precipice, in spite of the representations of Carathis and Morakanabad, who pointed out the hazard of its brink giving way, and the vicinity to the magician, that had so cruelly tormented him. Vathek derided all their remonstrances; and, having ordered a thousand flambeaux to be lighted, and directed his attendants to proceed in lighting more, lay down on the slippery margin, and attempted, by the help of this artificial splendour, to look through that gloom, which all the fires of the empyrean had been insufficient to pervade.

One while he fancied to himself voices arising from the depth of the gulph; at another, he seemed to distinguish the accents of the Indian; but all was no more than the hollow murmur of waters, and the din of the cataracts that rushed from steep to steep down the sides of the mountain.

Having passed the night in this cruel perturbation, the Caliph, at day-break, retired to his tent; where, without taking the least sustenance, he continued to doze till the dusk of evening began again to come on. He then resumed his vigils as before, and persevered in observing them for many nights together. At length, fatigued with so fruitless an employment, he sought relief from change. To this end, he sometimes paced with hasty strides across the plain; and, as he wildly gazed at the stars, reproached them with having deceived him; but, lo! on a sudden, the clear blue sky appeared streaked over with streams of blood, which reached from the valley even to the city of Samarah. As this awful phenomenon seemed to touch his tower, Vathek at first thought of repairing thither to view it more distinctly; but, feeling himself unable to advance, and being overcome with apprehension, he muffled up his face in the folds of his robe.

Terrifying as these prodigies were, this impression upon him was no more than momentary, and served only to stimulate his love of the marvellous. Instead, therefore, of returning to his palace, he persisted in the resolution of abiding where the Indian had vanished from his view. One night, however, while he was walking as usual on the plain, the moon and stars were eclipsed at once, and a total darkness ensued. The earth trembled beneath him, and a voice came forth, the voice of the Giaour, who, in accents more sonorous than thunder, thus addressed him: "Wouldest thou devote thyself to me? adore the terrestrial influences, and abjure Mahomet? On these conditions I will bring thee to the Palace of Subterranean Fire. There shalt thou behold, in immense depositories, the treasures which the stars have promised thee; and which will be conferred by those intelligences, whom thou shalt thus render propitious. It was from thence I brought my sabres, and it is there that Soliman Ben Daoud[17] reposes, surrounded by the talismans that control the world."

The astonished Caliph trembled as he answered, yet he answered in a style that shewed him to be no novice in preternatural adventures: "Where art thou? be present to my eyes; dissipate the gloom that perplexes me, and of which I deem thee the cause. After the many flambeaux I have burnt to discover thee, thou mayest, at least, grant a glimpse of thy horrible visage."—"Abjure then Mahomet!" replied the Indian, "and promise me full proofs of thy sincerity: otherwise, thou shalt never behold me again."

The unhappy Caliph, instigated by insatiable curiosity, lavished his promises in the utmost profusion. The sky immediately brightened; and, by the light of the planets, which seemed almost to blaze, Vathek beheld the earth open; and, at the extremity of a vast black chasm, a portal of ebony, before which stood the Indian, holding in his hand a golden key, which he sounded against the lock.

"How," cried Vathek, "can I descend to thee;—Come, take me, and instantly open the portal."—"Not so fast," replied the Indian, "impatient Caliph!—Know that I am parched with thirst, and cannot open this door, till my thirst be thoroughly appeased; I require the blood of fifty children. Take them from among the most beautiful sons of thy vizirs and great men; or, neither can my thirst nor thy curiosity be satisfied. Return to Samarah; procure for me this necessary libation; come back hither; throw it thyself into this chasm, and then shalt thou see!"

Having thus spoken, the Indian turned his back on the Caliph, who, incited by the suggestions of demons, resolved on the direful sacrifice.—He now pretended to have regained his tranquillity, and set out for Samarah amidst the acclamations of a people who still loved him, and forbore not to rejoice, when they believed him to have recovered his reason. So successfully did he conceal the emotion of his heart, that even Carathis and Morakanabad were equally deceived with the rest. Nothing was heard of but festivals and rejoicings. The fatal ball, which no tongue had hitherto ventured to mention, was brought on the tapis. A general laugh went round, though many, still smarting under the hands of the surgeon, from the hurts received in that memorable adventure, had no great reason for mirth.

The prevalence of this gay humour was not a little grateful to Vathek, who perceived how much it conduced to his project. He put on the appearance of affability to every one; but especially to his vizirs, and the grandees of his court, whom he failed not to regale with a sumptuous banquet; during which, he insensibly directed the conversation to the children of his guests. Having asked, with a good-natured air, which of them were blessed with the handsomest boys, every father at once asserted the pretensions of his own; and the contest imperceptibly grew so warm, that nothing could have withholden them from coming to blows, but their profound reverence for the person of the Caliph. Under the pretence, therefore, of reconciling the disputants, Vathek took upon him to decide; and, with this view, commanded the boys to be brought.

It was not long before a troop of these poor children made their appearance, all equipped by their fond mothers with such ornaments, as might give the greatest relief to their beauty, or most advantageously display the graces of their age. But, whilst this brilliant assemblage attracted the eyes and hearts of every one besides, the Caliph scrutinized each, in his turn, with a malignant avidity that passed for attention, and selected from their number the fifty whom he judged the Giaour would prefer.

With an equal shew of kindness as before, he proposed to celebrate a festival on the plain, for the entertainment of his young favourites, who, he said, ought to rejoice still more than all, at the restoration of his health, on account of the favours he intended for them.

The Caliph's proposal was received with the greatest delight, and soon published through Samarah. Litters, camels, and horses were prepared. Women and children, old men and young, every one placed himself as he chose. The cavalcade set forward, attended by all the confectioners in the city and its precincts; the populace, following on foot, composed an amazing crowd, and occasioned no little noise. All was joy; nor did any one call to mind, what most of them had suffered, when they lately travelled the road they were now passing so gaily.

The evening was serene, the air refreshing, the sky clear, and the flowers exhaled their fragrance. The beams of the declining sun, whose mild splendour reposed on the summit of the mountain, shed a glow of ruddy light over its green declivity, and the white flocks sporting upon it. No sounds were heard, save the murmurs of the four fountains; and the reeds and voices of shepherds calling to each other from different eminences.

The lovely innocents destined for the sacrifice, added not a little to the hilarity of the scene. They approached the plain full of sportiveness, some coursing butterflies, others culling flowers, or picking up the shining little pebbles that attracted their notice. At intervals they nimbly started from each other for the sake of being caught again, and mutually imparting a thousand caresses.

The dreadful chasm, at whose bottom the portal of ebony was

placed, began to appear at a distance. It looked like a black streak that divided the plain. Morakanabad and his companions, took it for some work which the Caliph had ordered. Unhappy men! little did they surmise for what it was destined. Vathek unwilling that they should examine it too nearly, stopped the procession, and ordered a spacious circle to be formed on this side, at some distance from the accursed chasm. The body-guard of eunuchs was detached, to measure out the lists intended for the games; and prepare the rings for the arrows of the young archers. The fifty competitors were soon stripped, and presented to the admiration of the spectators the suppleness and grace of their delicate limbs. Their eyes sparkled with a joy, which those of their fond parents reflected. Every one offered wishes for the little candidate nearest his heart, and doubted not of his being victorious. A breathless suspence awaited the contest of these amiable and innocent victims.

The Caliph, availing himself of the first moment to retire from the crowd, advanced towards the chasm; and there heard, yet not without shuddering, the voice of the Indian; who, gnashing his teeth, eagerly demanded: "Where are they?—Where are they?—perceivest thou not how my mouth waters?"—"Relentless Giaour!" answered Vathek, with emotion; "can nothing content thee but the massacre of these lovely victims? Ah! wert thou to behold their beauty, it must certainly move thy compassion."—"Perdition on thy compassion, babbler!" cried the Indian: "give them me; instantly give them, or, my portal shall be closed against thee for ever!"—"Not so loudly," replied the Caliph, blushing.—"I understand thee," returned the Giaour with the grin of an Ogre[18]; "thou wantest no presence of mind: I will, for a moment, forbear."

During this exquisite dialogue, the games went forward with all alacrity, and at length concluded, just as the twilight began to overcast the mountains. Vathek, who was still standing on the edge of the chasm, called out, with all his might:—"Let my fifty little favourites approach me, separately; and let them come in the order of their success. To the first, I will give my diamond bracelet; to the second, my collar of emeralds; to the third, my aigret of rubies; to the fourth, my girdle of topazes; and to the rest, each a part of my dress, even down to my slippers."

This declaration was received with reiterated acclamations; and all extolled the liberality of a prince, who would thus strip himself, for the amusement of his subjects, and the encouragement of the rising generation. The Caliph, in the meanwhile, undressed himself by degrees; and, raising his arm as high as he was able, made each of the prizes glitter in the air; but, whilst he delivered it, with one hand, to the child, who sprung forward to receive it; he, with the other, pushed the poor innocent into the gulph; where the Giaour, with a sullen muttering, incessantly repeated; "more! more!"

This dreadful device was executed with so much dexterity, that the boy who was approaching him, remained unconscious of the fate of his forerunner; and, as to the spectators, the shades of evening, together with their distance, precluded them from perceiving any object distinctly. Vathek, having in this manner thrown in the last of the fifty; and, expecting that the Giaour, on receiving him, would have presented the key; already fancied himself, as great as Soliman, and, consequently, above being amenable for what he had done:—when, to his utter amazement, the chasm closed, and the ground became as entire as the rest of the plain.

No language could express his rage and despair. He execrated the perfidy of the Indian; loaded him with the most infamous invectives; and stamped with his foot, as resolving to be heard. He persisted in this till his strength failed him; and, then, fell on the earth like one void of sense. His vizirs and grandees, who were nearer than the rest, supposed him, at first, to be sitting on the grass, at play with their amiable children; but, at length, prompted by doubt, they advanced towards the spot, and found the Caliph alone, who wildly demanded what they wanted? "Our children! our children!" cried they. "It is, assuredly, pleasant," said he, "to make me accountable for accidents. Your children, while at play, fell from the precipice, and I should have experienced their fate, had I not suddenly started back."

At these words, the fathers of the fifty boys cried out aloud; the mothers repeated their exclamations an octave higher; whilst the rest, without knowing the cause, soon drowned the voices of both, with still louder lamentations of their own. "Our Caliph," said they, and the report soon circulated, "our Caliph has played us this trick, to gratify his accursed Giaour. Let us punish him for perfidy! let us avenge ourselves! let us avenge the blood of the innocent! let us throw this cruel prince into the gulph that is near, and let his name be mentioned no more!"

At this rumour and these menaces, Carathis, full of consternation, hastened to Morakanabad, and said: "Vizir, you have lost two beautiful boys, and must necessarily be the most afflicted of fathers; but you are virtuous; save your master."—"I will brave every hazard," replied the vizir, "to rescue him from his present danger; but, afterwards, will abandon him to his fate. Bababalouk," continued he, "put yourself at the head of your eunuchs: disperse the mob, and, if possible, bring back this unhappy prince to his palace." Bababalouk and his fraternity, felicitating each other in a low voice on their having been spared the cares as well as the honour of paternity, obeyed the mandate of the vizir; who, seconding their exertions, to the utmost of his power, at length, accomplished his generous enterprize; and retired, as he resolved, to lament at his leisure.

No sooner had the Caliph re-entered his palace, than Carathis commanded the doors to be fastened; but, perceiving the tumult to be still violent, and hearing the imprecations which resounded from all quarters, she said to her son: "Whether the populace be right or wrong, it behoves you to provide for your safety; let us retire to your own apartment, and, from thence, through the subterranean passage, known only to ourselves, into your tower: there, with the assistance of the mutes[19] who never leave it, we may be able to make a powerful resistance. Bababalouk, supposing us to be still in the palace, will guard its avenues, for his own sake; and we shall soon find, without the counsels of that blubberer Morakanabad, what expedient may be the best to adopt."

Vathek, without making the least reply, acquiesced in his mother's proposal, and repeated as he went: "Nefarious Giaour! where art thou? hast thou not yet devoured those poor children? where are thy sabres? thy golden key? thy talismans?"—Carathis, who guessed from these interrogations a part of the truth, had no difficulty to apprehend, in getting at the whole as soon as he should be a little composed in his tower. This Princess was so far from being influenced by scruples, that she was as wicked, as woman could be; which is not saying a little; for the sex pique themselves on their superiority, in every competition. The recital of the Caliph, therefore, occasioned neither terror nor surprize to his mother: she felt no emotion but from the promises of the Giaour, and said to her son: "This Giaour, it must be confessed, is somewhat sanguinary in his taste; but, the terrestrial powers are always terrible; nevertheless, what the one hath promised, and the others can confer, will prove a sufficient indemnification. No crimes should be thought too dear for such a reward: forbear, then, to revile the Indian; you have not fulfilled the conditions to which his services are annexed: for instance; is not a sacrifice to the subterranean Genii required? and should we not be prepared to offer it as soon as the tumult is subsided? This charge I will take on myself, and have no doubt of succeeding, by means of your treasures, which as there are now so many others in store, may, without fear, be exhausted." Accordingly, the Princess, who possessed the most consummate skill in the art of persuasion, went immediately back through the subterranean passage; and, presenting herself to the populace, from a window of the palace, began to harangue them with all the address of which she was mistress; whilst Bababalouk, showered money from both hands amongst the crowd, who by these united means were soon appeased. Every person retired to his home, and Carathis returned to the tower.

Prayer at break of day[20] was announced, when Carathis and Vathek ascended the steps, which led to the summit of the tower; where they remained for some time though the weather was lowering and wet. This impending gloom corresponded with their malignant dispositions; but when the sun began to break through the clouds, they ordered a pavilion to be raised, as a screen against the intrusion of his beams. The Caliph, over-come with fatigue, sought refreshment from repose; at the same time, hoping that significant dreams might attend on his slumbers; whilst the indefatigable Carathis, followed by a party of her mutes, descended to prepare whatever she judged proper, for the oblation of the approaching night.

By secret stairs, contrived within the thickness of the wall, and known only to herself and her son, she first repaired to the mysterious recesses in which were deposited the mummies[21] that had been wrested from the catacombs of the ancient Pharaohs. Of these she ordered several to be taken. From thence, she resorted to a gallery; where, under the guard of fifty female negroes mute and blind of the right eye, were preserved the oil of the most venomous serpents; rhinoceros' horns; and woods of a subtile and penetrating odour, procured from the interior of the Indies, together with a thousand other horrible rarities. This collection had been formed for a purpose like the present, by Carathis herself; from a presentiment, that she might one day, enjoy some intercourse with the infernal powers: to whom she had ever been passionately attached, and to whose taste she was no stranger.

To familiarize herself the better with the horrors in view, the Princess remained in the company of her negresses, who squinted in the most amiable manner from the only eye they had; and leered with exquisite delight, at the sculls and skeletons which Carathis had drawn forth from her cabinets: all of them making the most frightful contortions and uttering such shrill chatterings, that the Princess stunned by them and suffocated by the potency of the exhalations, was forced to quit the gallery, after stripping it of a part of its abominable treasures.

Whilst she was thus occupied, the Caliph, who instead of the visions he expected, had acquired in these unsubstantial regions a voracious appetite, was greatly provoked at the mutes. For having totally forgotten their deafness, he had impatiently asked them for food; and seeing them regardless of his demand, he began to cuff, pinch, and bite them, till Carathis arrived to terminate a scene so indecent, to the great content of these miserable creatures: "Son! what means all this?" said she, panting for breath. "I thought I heard as I came up, the shrieks of a thousand bats, torn from their crannies in the recesses of a cavern; and it was the outcry only of these poor mutes, whom you were so unmercifully abusing. In truth, you but ill deserve the admirable provision I have brought you."—"Give it me instantly," exclaimed the Caliph; "I am perishing for hunger!"— "As to that," answered she, "you must have an excellent stomach if it can digest what I have brought."—"Be quick," replied the Caliph;—"but, oh heavens! what horrors! what do you intend?" "Come; come;" returned Carathis, "be not so squeamish; but help me to arrange every thing properly; and you shall see that, what you reject with such symptoms of disgust, will soon complete your felicity. Let us get ready the pile, for the sacrifice of to-night; and think not of eating, till that is performed: know you not, that all solemn rites ought to be preceded by a rigorous abstinence?"

The Caliph, not daring to object, abandoned himself to grief and the wind that ravaged his entrails, whilst his mother went forward with the requisite operations. Phials of serpents' oil, mummies, and bones, were soon set in order on the balustrade of the tower. The pile began to rise; and in three hours was twenty cubits high. At length darkness approached, and Carathis, having stripped herself to her inmost garment, clapped her hands in an impulse of ecstacy; the mutes followed her example; but Vathek, extenuated with hunger and impatience, was unable to support himself, and fell down in a swoon. The sparks had already kindled the dry wood; the venomous oil burst into a thousand blue flames; the mummies, dissolving, emitted a thick dun vapour; and the rhinoceros' horns, beginning to consume; all together diffused such a stench, that the Caliph, recovering, started from his trance, and gazed wildly on the scene in full blaze around him. The oil gushed forth in a plenitude of streams; and the negresses, who supplied it without intermission, united their cries to those of the Princess. At last, the fire became so violent, and the flames reflected from the polished marble so dazzling, that the Caliph, unable to withstand the heat and the blaze, effected his escape; and took shelter under the imperial standard.

In the mean time, the inhabitants of Samarah, scared at the

light which shone over the city, arose in haste; ascended their roofs; beheld the tower on fire, and hurried, half naked to the square. Their love for their sovereign immediately awoke; and, apprehending him in danger of perishing in his tower, their whole thoughts were occupied with the means of his safety. Morakanabad flew from his retirement, wiped away his tears, and cried out for water like the rest. Bababalouk, whose olfactory nerves were more familiarized to magical odours, readily conjecturing, that Carathis was engaged in her favourite amusements, strenuously exhorted them not to be alarmed. Him, however, they treated as an old poltroon, and styled him a rascally traitor. The camels and dromedaries were advancing with water; but, no one knew by which way to enter the tower. Whilst the populace was obstinate in forcing the doors, a violent north-east wind drove an immense volume of flame against them. At first, they recoiled, but soon came back with redoubled zeal. At the same time, the stench of the horns and mummies increasing, most of the crowd fell backward in a state of suffocation. Those that kept their feet, mutually wondered at the cause of the smell; and admonished each other to retire. Morakanabad, more sick than the rest, remained in a piteous condition. Holding his nose with one hand, every one persisted in his efforts with the other to burst open the doors and obtain admission. A hundred and forty of the strongest and most resolute, at length accomplished their purpose. Having gained the stair-case, by their violent exertions, they attained a great height in a quarter of an hour.

Carathis, alarmed at the signs of her mutes, advanced to the stair-case; went down a few steps, and heard several voices calling out from below: "You shall, in a moment have water!" Being rather alert, considering her age, she presently regained the top of the tower; and bade her son suspend the sacrifice for some minutes; adding,—"We shall soon be enabled to render it more grateful. Certain dolts of your subjects, imagining no doubt that we were on fire, have been rash enough to break through those doors, which had hitherto remained inviolate; for the sake of bringing up water. They are very kind, you must allow, so soon to forget the wrongs you have done them; but that is of little moment. Let us offer them to the Giaour,—let them come up; our mutes, who neither want strength nor experience, will soon dispatch them; exhausted as they are, with fatigue."—"Be it so," answered the Caliph, "provided we finish, and I dine." In fact, these good people, out of breath from ascending fifteen hundred stairs in such haste; and chagrined, at having spilt by the way, the water they had taken, were no sooner arrived at the top, than the blaze of the flames, and the fumes of the mummies, at once overpowered their senses. It was a pity! for they beheld not the agreeable smile, with which the mutes and negresses adjusted the cord to their necks: these amiable personages rejoiced, however, no less at the scene. Never before had the ceremony of strangling been performed with so much facility. They all fell, without the least resistance or struggle: so that Vathek, in the space of a few moments, found himself surrounded by the dead bodies of the most faithful of his subjects; all which were thrown on the top of the pile. Carathis, whose presence of mind never forsook her, perceiving that she had carcasses sufficient to complete her oblation, commanded the chains to be stretched across the stair-case, and the iron doors barricadoed, that no more might come up.

No sooner were these orders obeyed, than the tower shook; the dead bodies vanished in the flames; which, at once, changed from a swarthy crimson, to a bright rose colour: an ambient vapour emitted the most exquisite fragrance; the marble columns rang with harmonious sounds, and the liquified horns diffused a delicious perfume. Carathis, in transports, anticipated the success of her enterprize; whilst her mutes and negresses, to whom these sweets had given the cholic, retired grumbling to their cells.

Scarcely were they gone, when, instead of the pile, horns, mummies and ashes, the Caliph both saw and felt, with a degree of pleasure which he could not express, a table, covered with the most magnificent repast: flaggons of wine, and vases of exquisite sherbet reposing on snow. He availed himself, without scruple, of such an entertainment; and had already laid hands on a lamb stuffed with pistachios, whilst Carathis was privately drawing from a fillagreen urn, a parchment[22] that seemed to be endless; and which had escaped the notice of her son. Totally occupied in gratifying an importunate appetitite, he left her to peruse it without interruption; which having finished, she said to him, in an authoritative tone, "Put an end to your gluttony, and hear the splendid promises with which you are favoured!" She then read, as follows: "Vathek, my well-beloved, thou hast surpassed my hopes: my nostrils have been regaled by the savour of thy mummies, thy horns; and, still more by the lives, devoted on the pile. At the full of the moon, cause the bands of thy musicians, and thy tymbals, to be heard; depart from thy palace, surrounded by all the pageants of majesty; thy most faithful slaves, thy best beloved wives; thy most magnificent litters; thy richest loaden camels; and set forward on thy way to Istakhar[23]. There, I await thy coming: that is the region of wonders: there shalt thou receive the diadem of Gian Ben Gian; the talismans of Soliman[24]; and the treasures of the pre-adamite sultans[25]: there shalt thou be solaced with all kinds of delight.—But, beware how thou enterest any dwelling[26] on thy route; or thou shalt feel the effects of my anger."

The Caliph, notwithstanding his habitual luxury, had never

before dined with so much satisfaction. He gave full scope to the joy of these golden tidings; and betook himself to drinking anew. Carathis, whose antipathy to wine was by no means insuperable, failed not to pledge him at every bumper he ironically quaffed to the health of Mahomet[27]. This infernal liquor completed their impious temerity, and prompted them to utter a profusion of blasphemies. They gave a loose to their wit, at the expense of the ass of Balaam, the dog of the seven sleepers, and the other animals admitted into the paradise of Mahomet[28]. In this sprightly humour, they descended the fifteen hundred stairs, diverting themselves as they went, at the anxious faces they saw on the square, through the barbacans and loopholes of the tower; and, at length, arrived at the royal apartments, by the subterranean passage. Bababalouk was parading to and fro, and issuing his mandates, with great pomp to the eunuchs; who were snuffing the lights and painting the eyes of the Circassians[29]. No sooner did he catch sight of the Caliph and his mother, than he exclaimed, "Hah! you have, then, I perceive, escaped from the flames: I was not, however, altogether out of doubt."—"Of what moment is it to us what you thought, or think?" cried Carathis: "go; speed; tell Morakanabad that we immediately want him: and take care, not to stop by the way, to make your insipid reflections."

Morakanabad delayed not to obey the summons; and was received by Vathek and his mother, with great solemnity. They told him, with an air of composure and commiseration, that the fire at the top of the tower was extinguished; but that it had cost the lives of the brave people who sought to assist them.

"Still more misfortunes!" cried Morakanabad, with a sigh. "Ah, commander of the faithful, our holy prophet is certainly irritated against us! it behoves you to appease him."—"We will appease him, hereafter!" replied the Caliph, with a smile, that augured nothing of good. "You will have leisure sufficient for your supplications, during my absence: for this country is the bane of my health. I am disgusted with the mountain of the four fountains, and am resolved to go and drink of the stream of Rocnabad[30]. I long to refresh myself, in the delightful vallies which it waters. Do you, with the advice of my mother, govern my dominions, and take care to supply whatever her experiments may demand: for, you well know, that our tower abounds in materials for the advancement of science."

The tower but ill suited Morakanabad's taste. Immense treasures had been lavished upon it; and nothing had he ever seen carried thither but female negroes, mutes and abominable drugs. Nor did he know well what to think of Carathis, who, like a cameleon, could assume all possible colours. Her cursed eloquence had often driven the poor mussulman to his last shifts. He considered, however, that if she possessed but few good qualities, her son had still fewer; and that the alternative, on the whole, would be in her favour. Consoled, therefore, with this reflection; he went, in good spirits, to soothe the populace, and make the proper arrangements for his master's journey.

Vathek, to conciliate the Spirits of the subterranean palace, resolved that his expedition should be uncommonly splendid. With this view he confiscated, on all sides, the property of his subjects; whilst his worthy mother stripped the seraglios she visited, of the gems they contained. She collected all the sempstresses* and embroiderers of Samarah and other cities, to the distance of sixty leagues; to prepare pavilions, palanquins; sofas, canopies, and litters for the train of the monarch. There was not left, in Masulipatan, a single piece of chintz; and so much muslin had been brought up to dress out Bababalouk and the other

*Seamstresses.

black eunuchs, that there remained not an ell of it in the whole Irak of Babylon.

During these preparations, Carathis, who never lost sight of her great object, which was to obtain favour with the powers of darkness, made select parties of the fairest and most delicate ladies of the city: but in the midst of their gaiety, she contrived to introduce vipers amongst them, and to break pots of scorpions under the table. They all bit to a wonder, and Carathis would have left her friends to die, were it not that, to fill up the time, she now and then amused herself in curing their wounds, with an excellent anodyne of her own invention: for this good Princess abhorred being indolent.

Vathek, who was not altogether so active as his mother, devoted his time to the sole gratification of his senses, in the palaces which were severally dedicated to them. He disgusted himself no more with the divan, or the mosque. One half of Samarah followed his example, whilst the other lamented the progress of corruption.

In the midst of these transactions, the embassy returned, which had been sent, in pious times, to Mecca. It consisted of the most reverend Moullahs[31] who had fulfilled their commission, and brought back one of those precious besoms* which are used to sweep the sacred Cahaba[32]: a present truly worthy of the greatest potentate on earth!

The Caliph happened at this instant to be engaged in an apartment by no means adapted to the reception of embassies. He heard the voice of Bababalouk, calling out from between the door and the tapestry that hung before it: "Here are the excellent Edris al Shafei, and the seraphic Al Mouhateddin, who have brought the besom from Mecca, and, with tears of

---

*A broom made of twigs tied to a stick.

joy, entreat they may present it to your majesty in person."—
"Let them bring the besom hither, it may be of use," said Vathek.
"How!" answered Bababalouk, half aloud and amazed. "Obey,"
replied the Caliph, "for it is my sovereign will; go instantly, van-
ish! for here will I receive the good folk who have thus filled
thee with joy."

The eunuch departed muttering, and bade the venerable
train attend him. A sacred rapture was diffused amongst these
reverend old men. Though fatigued with the length of their
expedition, they followed Bababalouk with an alertness almost
miraculous, and felt themselves highly flattered, as they swept
along the stately porticos, that the Caliph would not receive
them like ambassadors in ordinary in his hall of audience. Soon
reaching the interior of the harem (where, through blinds of
Persian, they perceived large soft eyes, dark and blue, that came
and went like lightning) penetrated with respect and wonder,
and full of their celestial mission, they advanced in procession
towards the small corridors that appeared to terminate in nothing, but, nevertheless, led to the cell where the Caliph expected
their coming.

"What! is the commander of the faithful sick?" said Edris al
Shafei, in a low voice to his companion?—"I rather think he is
in his oratory," answered Al Mouhateddin. Vathek, who heard
the dialogue, cried out:—"What imports it you, how I am
employed? approach without delay." They advanced, whilst the
Caliph, without shewing himself, put forth his hand from behind
the tapestry that hung before the door, and demanded of them
the besom. Having prostrated themselves as well as the corridor
would permit, and, even in a tolerable semicircle, the venerable
Al Shafei, drawing forth the besom from the embroidered and
perfumed scarves, in which it had been enveloped, and secured
from the profane gaze of vulgar eyes, arose from his associates,

and advanced, with an air of the most awful solemnity towards the supposed oratory; but, with what astonishment! with what horror was he seized!—Vathek, bursting out into a villainous laugh, snatched the besom from his trembling hand, and, fixing upon some cobwebs, that hung from the ceiling, gravely brushed them away till not a single one remained. The old men, overpowered with amazement, were unable to lift their beards from the ground: for, as Vathek had carelessly left the tapestry between them half drawn, they were witnesses of the whole transaction. Their tears bedewed the marble. Al Mouhateddin swooned through mortification and fatigue, whilst the Caliph, throwing himself backward on his seat, shouted, and clapped his hands without mercy. At last, addressing himself to Bababalouk!—"My dear black," said he, "go, regale these pious poor souls, with my good wine from Shiraz[33], since they can boast of having seen more of my palace than any one besides." Having said this, he threw the besom in their face, and went to enjoy the laugh with Carathis. Bababalouk did all in his power to console the ambassadors; but the two most infirm expired on the spot: the rest were carried to their beds, from whence, being heart-broken with sorrow and shame, they never arose.

The succeeding night, Vathek, attended by his mother, ascended the tower to see if every thing were ready for his journey: for, he had great faith in the influence of the stars. The planets appeared in their most favourable aspects. The Caliph, to enjoy so flattering a sight, supped gaily on the roof; and fancied that he heard, during his repast, loud shouts of laughter resound through the sky, in a manner, that inspired the fullest assurance.

All was in motion at the palace; lights were kept burning through the whole of the night: the sound of implements, and of artizans finishing their work; the voices of women, and their

guardians, who sung at their embroidery: all conspired to interrupt the stillness of nature, and infinitely delighted the heart of
Vathek who imagined himself going in triumph to sit upon the
throne of Soliman. The people were not less satisfied than himself: all assisted to accelerate the moment, which should rescue
them from the wayward caprices of so extravagant a master.

The day preceding the departure of this infatuated Prince,
was employed by Carathis, in repeating to him the decrees of
the mysterious parchment; which she had thoroughly gotten by
heart; and, in recommending him, not to enter the habitation of
any one by the way: "for, well thou knowest," added she, "how
liquorish* thy taste is after good dishes and young damsels; let
me, therefore, enjoin thee, to be content with thy old cooks,
who are the best in the world: and not to forget that, in thy
ambulatory seraglio, there are at least three dozen of pretty faces
which Bababalouk had not yet unveiled. I myself have a great
desire to watch over thy conduct, and visit the subterranean palace, which, no doubt, contains whatever can interest persons,
like us. There is nothing so pleasing as retiring to caverns: my
taste for dead bodies, and every thing like mummy is decided:
and, I am confident, thou wilt see the most exquisite of their
kind. Forget me not then, but the moment thou art in posses-
sion of the talismans which are to open the way to the mineral
kingdoms and the centre of the earth itself, fail not to dispatch
some trusty genius to take me and my cabinet: for the oil of the
serpents I have pinched to death will be a pretty present to the
Giaour who cannot but be charmed with such dainties."

Scarcely had Carathis ended this edifying discourse, when
the sun, setting behind the mountain of the four fountains, gave
place to the rising moon. This planet, being that evening at full,

---

*An archaic form of "lecherous."

appeared of unusual beauty and magnitude, in the eyes of the women, the eunuchs and the pages who were all impatient to set forward. The city re-echoed with shouts of joy, and flourishing of trumpets. Nothing was visible, but plumes, nodding on pavilions, and aigrets shining in the mild lustre of the moon. The spacious square resembled an immense parterre variegated with the most stately tulips of the east[34].

Arrayed in the robes which were only worn at the most distinguished ceremonials, and supported by his vizir and Bababalouk, the Caliph descended the great staircase of the tower in the sight of all his people. He could not forbear pausing, at intervals, to admire the superb appearance which every where courted his view: whilst the whole multitude, even to the camels with their sumptuous burthens, knelt down before him. For some time a general stillness prevailed, which nothing happened to disturb, but the shrill screams of some eunuchs in the rear. These vigilant guards, having remarked certain cages of the ladies[35] swagging* somewhat awry, and discovered that a few adventurous gallants had contrived to get in, soon dislodged the enraptured culprits and consigned them, with good commendations, to the surgeons of the serail. The majesty of so magnificent a spectacle, was not, however, violated by incidents like these. Vathek, meanwhile, saluted the moon with an idolatrous air, that neither pleased Morakanabad, nor the doctors of the law, any more than the vizirs and grandees of his court, who were all assembled to enjoy the last view of their sovereign.

At length, the clarions and trumpets from the top of the tower, announced the prelude of departure. Though the instruments were in unison with each other, yet a singular dissonance was blended with their sounds. This proceeded from

---

*Swaying to and fro.

Carathis who was singing her direful orisons to the Giaour, whilst the negresses and mutes supplied thorough base, without articulating a word. The good Mussulmans fancied that they heard the sullen hum of those nocturnal insects, which presage evil; and importuned Vathek to beware how he ventured his sacred person.

On a given signal, the great standard of the Califat was displayed; twenty thousand lances shone around it; and the Caliph, treading royally on the cloth of gold, which had been spread for his feet, ascended his litter, amidst the general acclamations of his subjects.

The expedition commenced with the utmost order and so entire a silence, that, even the locusts were heard from the thickets on the plain of Catoul[36]. Gaiety and good humour prevailing, they made full six leagues before the dawn; and the morning star was still glittering in the firmament, when the whole of this numerous train had halted on the banks of the Tigris, where they encamped to repose for the rest of the day.

The three days that followed were spent in the same manner; but, on the fourth, the heavens looked angry; lightnings broke forth, in frequent flashes; re-echoing peals of thunder succeeded; and the trembling Circassians clung with all their might, to their ugly guardians. The Caliph himself, was greatly inclined to take shelter in the large town of Ghulchissar, the governor of which, came forth to meet him, and tendered every kind of refreshment the place could supply. But, having examined his tablets, he suffered the rain to soak him, almost to the bone, notwithstanding the importunity of his first favourites. Though he began to regret the palace of the senses; yet, he lost not sight of his enterprize, and his sanguine expectation confirmed his resolution. His geographers were ordered to attend him; but, the weather proved so terrible that these poor people exhibited a lamentable appearance: and their maps of the different countries spoiled by the rain, were in a still worse plight than themselves. As no long journey had been undertaken since the time of Haroun al Raschid, every one was ignorant which way to turn; and Vathek, though well versed in the course of the heavens, no longer knew his situation on earth. He thundered even louder than the elements; and muttered forth certain hints of the bow-string which were not very soothing to literary ears. Disgusted at the toilsome weariness of the way, he determined to cross over the craggy heights and follow the guidance of a peasant, who undertook to bring him, in four days, to Rocnabad. Remonstrances were all to no purpose; his resolution was fixed.

The females and eunuchs uttered shrill wailings at the sight of the precipices below them, and the dreary prospects that opened, in the vast gorges of the mountains. Before they could reach the ascent of the steepest rock, night overtook them, and a boisterous tempest arose, which, having rent the awnings of the palanquins and cages, exposed to the raw gusts the poor ladies within, who had never before felt so piercing a cold. The dark clouds that overcast the face of the sky deepened the horrors of this disastrous night, insomuch that nothing could be heard distinctly, but the mewling of pages and lamentations of sultanas.

To increase the general misfortune, the frightful uproar of wild beasts resounded at a distance; and there were soon perceived in the forest they were skirting, the glaring of eyes, which could belong only to devils or tigers. The pioneers, who, as well as they could, had marked out a track; and a part of the advanced guard, were devoured, before they had been in the least apprized of their danger. The confusion that prevailed was extreme. Wolves, tigers, and other carnivorous animals, invited by the howling of their companions, flocked together from every quarter. The crashing of bones was heard on all sides, and

a fearful rush of wings over head; for now vultures also began to
be of the party.

The terror at length reached the main body of the troops
which surrounded the monarch and his harem at the distance
of two leagues from the scene. Vathek (voluptuously reposed
in his capacious litter upon cushions of silk, with two little
pages[37] beside him of complexions more fair than the enamel
of Franguistan,* who were occupied in keeping off flies) was
soundly asleep, and contemplating in his dreams the treasures
of Soliman. The shrieks however of his wives, awoke him with a
start; and, instead of the Giaour with his key of gold, he beheld
Bababalouk full of consternation. "Sire," exclaimed this good
servant of the most potent of monarchs, "misfortune is arrived
at its height, wild beasts, who entertain no more reverence for
your sacred person, than for a dead ass, have beset your camels and their drivers; thirty of the most richly laden are already
become their prey, as well as your confectioners, your cooks[38],
and purveyors: and, unless our holy Prophet should protect us,
we shall have all eaten our last meal." At the mention of eating,
the Caliph lost all patience. He began to bellow, and even beat
himself (for there was no seeing in the dark). The rumour every
instant increased; and Bababalouk, finding no good could be
done with his master, stopped both his ears against the hurly-
burly of the harem, and called out aloud: "Come, ladies, and
brothers! all hands to work: strike light in a moment! never shall
it be said, that the commander of the faithful served to regale
these infidel brutes." Though there wanted not in this bevy of
beauties, a sufficient number of capricious and wayward; yet,
on the present occasion, they were all compliance. Fires were
visible, in a twinkling, in all their cages. Ten thousand torches

---

*Western Europe.

were lighted[39] at once. The Caliph, himself, seized a large one of wax: every person followed his example; and, by kindling ropes ends, dipped in oil and fastened on poles, an amazing blaze was spread. The rocks were covered with the splendour of sun-shine. The trails of sparks, wafted by the wind, communicated to the dry fern, of which there was plenty. Serpents were observed to crawl forth from their retreats, with amazement and hissings; whilst the horses snorted, stamped the ground, tossed their noses in the air, and plunged about, without mercy.

One of the forests of cedar that bordered their way, took fire[40]; and the branches that overhung the path, extending their flames to the muslins and chintzes, which covered the cages of the ladies obliged them to jump out, at the peril of their necks. Vathek, who vented on the occasion a thousand blasphemies, was himself compelled to touch, with his sacred feet, the naked earth.

Never had such an incident happened before. Full of mortification, shame, and despondence, and not knowing how to walk, the ladies fell into the dirt. "Must I go on foot!" said one: "Must I wet my feet!" cried another: "Must I soil my dress!" asked a third: "Execrable Bababalouk!" exclaimed all: "Outcast of hell! what hast thou to do with torches! Better were it to be eaten by tigers, than to fall into our present condition! we are for ever undone! Not a porter is there in the army nor a currier of camels; but hath seen some part of our bodies; and, what is worse, our very faces![41]" On saying this, the most bashful amongst them hid their foreheads on the ground, whilst such as had more boldness flew at Bababalouk; but he, well apprized of their humour and not wanting in shrewdness, betook himself to his heels along with his comrades, all dropping their torches and striking their tymbals.

It was not less light than in the brightest of the dog-days, and the weather was hot in proportion; but how degrading was the spectacle, to behold the Caliph bespattered, like an ordinary mortal! As the exercise of his faculties seemed to be suspended, one of his Ethiopian wives (for he delighted in variety) clasped him in her arms; threw him upon her shoulder, like a sack of dates, and, finding that the fire was hemming them in, set off, with no small expedition, considering the weight of her burden. The other ladies, who had just learnt the use of their feet, followed her; their guards galloped after; and the camel-drivers brought up the rear, as fast as their charge would permit.

They soon reached the spot, where the wild beasts had commenced the carnage, but which they had too much good sense not to leave at the approaching of the tumult, having made besides a most luxurious supper. Bababalouk, nevertheless, seized on a few of the plumpest, which were unable to budge from the place, and began to flea them with admirable adroitness. The cavalcade having proceeded so far from the conflagration, that the heat felt rather grateful than violent, it was, immediately, resolved on to halt. The tattered chintzes were picked up; the scraps, left by the wolves and tigers, interred; and vengeance was taken on some dozens of vultures, that were too much glutted to rise on the wing. The camels, which had been left unmolested to make sal ammoniac,* being numbered; and the ladies once more inclosed in their cages; the imperial tent was pitched on the levellest ground they could find.

Vathek, reposing upon a mattress of down, and tolerably recovered from the jolting of the Ethiopian, who, to his feelings, seemed the roughest trotting jade he had hitherto mounted, called out for something to eat. But, alas! those delicate cakes,

---

*Sal ammoniac, ammonium chloride, is a salt used in older times for cleaning and baking. It is found in the dung of camels. Therefore, the narrator is describing a "rest stop" for the camels.

which had been baked in silver ovens, for his royal mouth[42]; those rich manchets;* amber comfits;† flaggons of Schiraz wine; porcelain vases of snow; and grapes from the banks of the Tigris[43]; were all irremediably lost!—And nothing had Bababalouk to present in their stead, but a roasted wolf; vultures à la daube; aromatic herbs of the most acrid poignancy; rotten truffles; boiled thistles: and such other wild plants, as must ulcerate the throat and parch up the tongue. Nor was he better provided, in the article of drink: for he could procure nothing to accompany these irritating viands, but a few phials of abominable brandy which had been secreted by the scullions in their slippers. Vathek made wry faces at so savage a repast; and Bababalouk answered them, with shrugs and contortions. The Caliph, however, eat with tolerable appetite; and fell into a nap, that lasted six hours.

The splendour of the sun, reflected from the white cliffs of the mountains, in spite of the curtains that inclosed Vathek, at length disturbed his repose. He awoke, terrified; and stung to the quick by wormwood-colour flies, which emitted from their wings a suffocating stench. The miserable monarch was perplexed how to act; though his wits were not idle, in seeking expedients, whilst Bababalouk lay snoring, amidst a swarm of those insects that busily thronged, to pay court to his nose. The little pages, famished with hunger, had dropped their fans on the ground; and exerted their dying voices, in bitter reproaches on the Caliph; who now, for the first time, heard the language of truth.

Thus stimulated, he renewed his imprecations against the Giaour; and bestowed upon Mahomet some soothing expressions. "Where am I?" cried he: "What are these dreadful rocks?

---

*A yeast bread made from wheat.
†Sugar-coated nuts or fruits.

these valleys of darkness! are we arrived at the horrible Kaf[44]!
is the Simurgh[45] coming to pluck out my eyes, as a punishment
for undertaking this impious enterprize!" Having said this he
turned himself towards an outlet in the side of his pavilion, but,
alas! what objects occurred to his view? on one side, a plain of
black sand that appeared to be unbounded; and, on the other,
perpendicular crags, bristled over with those abominable thistles, which had, so severely, lacerated his tongue. He fancied,
however, that he perceived, amongst the brambles and briars,
some gigantic flowers but was mistaken: for, these were only the
dangling palampores and variegated tatters of his gay retinue. As
there were several clefts in the rock from whence water seemed
to have flowed, Vathek applied his ear with the hope of catching
the sound of some latent torrent; but could only distinguish the
low murmurs of his people who were repining at their journey,
and complaining for the want of water. "To what purpose," asked
they, "have we been brought hither? hath our Caliph another
tower to build? or have the relentless afrits[46], whom Carathis so
much loves, fixed their abode in this place?"

At the name of Carathis, Vathek recollected the tablets he had
received from his mother; who assured him, they were fraught
with preternatural qualities[47], and advised him to consult them,
as emergencies might require. Whilst he was engaged in turning
them over, he heard a shout of joy, and a loud clapping of hands.
The curtains of his pavilion were soon drawn back and he beheld
Bababalouk, followed by a troop of his favourites, conducting
two dwarfs[48] each a cubit high; who brought between them a
large basket of melons, oranges, and pomegranates. They were
singing in the sweetest tones the words that follow: "We dwell
on the top of these rocks, in a cabin of rushes and canes; the
eagles envy us our nest: a small spring supplies us with water
for the Abdest, and we daily repeat prayers[49], which the Prophet

approves. We love you, O commander of the faithful! our master, the good Emir Fakreddin, loves you also: he reveres, in your person, the vicegerent of Mahomet. Little as we are, in us he confides: he knows our hearts to be as good, as our bodies are contemptible; and hath placed us here to aid those who are bewildered on these dreary mountains. Last night, whilst we were occupied within our cell in reading the holy Koran, a sudden hurricane blew out our lights, and rocked our habitation. For two whole hours, a palpable darkness prevailed; but we heard sounds at a distance, which we conjectured to proceed from the bells of a Cafila[50], passing over the rocks. Our ears were soon filled with deplorable shrieks, frightful roarings, and the sound of tymbals. Chilled with terror, we concluded that the Deggial[51], with his exterminating angels, had sent forth his plagues on the earth. In the midst of these melancholy reflections, we perceived flames of the deepest red, glow in the horizon; and found ourselves, in a few moments, covered with flakes of fire. Amazed at so strange an appearance, we took up the volume dictated by the blessed intelligence, and, kneeling, by the light of the fire that surrounded us, we recited the verse which says: "Put no trust in any thing but the mercy of Heaven: there is no help, save in the holy Prophet: the mountain of Kaf, itself, may tremble; it is the power of Alla only, that cannot be moved." After having pronounced these words, we felt consolation, and our minds were hushed into a sacred repose. Silence ensued, and our ears clearly distinguished a voice in the air, saying: "Servants of my faithful servant! go down to the happy valley of Fakreddin: tell him that an illustrious opportunity now offers to satiate the thirst of his hospitable heart. The commander of true believers is, this day, bewildered amongst these mountains and stands in need of thy aid."—We obeyed, with joy, the angelic mission; and our master, filled with pious zeal, hath culled, with his own hands, these melons, oranges, and pomegranates. He is following us, with a hundred dromedaries, laden with the purest waters of his fountains; and is coming to kiss the fringe of your consecrated robe, and implore you to enter his humble habitation which, placed amidst these barren wilds, resembles an emerald set in lead." The dwarfs, having ended their address, remained still standing, and, with hands crossed upon their bosoms, preserved a respectful silence.

Vathek, in the midst of this curious harangue, seized the basket; and, long before it was finished, the fruits had dissolved in his mouth. As he continued to eat, his piety increased; and, in the same breath, he recited his prayers and called for the Koran and sugar[52].

Such was the state of his mind, when the tablets, which were thrown by, at the approach of the dwarfs, again attracted his eye. He took them up; but was ready to drop on the ground, when he beheld in large red characters[53] inscribed by Carathis, these words; which were, indeed, enough to make him tremble; "Beware of old doctors and their puny messengers of but one cubit high: distrust their pious frauds; and, instead of eating their melons, empale on a spit the bearers of them. Shouldest thou be such a fool as to visit them, the portal of the subterranean palace will shut in thy face with such force, as shall shake thee asunder: thy body shall be spit upon[54], and bats will nestle in thy belly.[55]"

"To what tends this ominous rhapsody?" cries the Caliph: "and must I then perish in these deserts, with thirst; whilst I may refresh myself in the delicious valley of melons and cucumbers?—Accursed be the Giaour with his portal of ebony! he hath made me dance attendance, too long already. Besides, who shall prescribe laws to me?—I, forsooth, must not enter any one's habitation! Be it so: but, what one can I enter, that is

not my own!" Bababalouk, who lost not a syllable of this soliloquy, applauded it with all his heart; and the ladies, for the first
time, agreed with him in opinion.

The dwarfs were entertained, caressed, and seated, with
great ceremony, on little cushions of satin. The symmetry of
their persons was a subject of admiration; not an inch of them
was suffered to pass unexamined. Knick-nacks and dainties
were offered in profusion; but all were declined, with respectful gravity. They climbed up the sides of the Caliph's seat;
and, placing themselves each on one of his shoulders, began
to whisper prayers in his ears. Their tongues quivered, like
aspen leaves; and the patience of Vathek was almost exhausted,
when the acclamations of the troops announced the approach
of Fakreddin, who was come with a hundred old grey-beards,
and as many Korans and dromedaries. They instantly set about
their ablutions, and began to repeat the Bismillah[56]. Vathek, to
get rid of these officious monitors, followed their example; for
his hands were burning.

The good emir, who was punctiliously religious, and likewise
a great dealer in compliments, made an harangue five times more
prolix and insipid than his little harbingers had already delivered.
The Caliph, unable any longer to refrain, exclaimed: "For the love
of Mahomet, my dear Fakreddin, have done! let us proceed to your
valley, and enjoy the fruits that Heaven hath vouchsafed you." The
hint of proceeding, put all into motion. The venerable attendants
of the emir set forward, somewhat slowly; but Vathek, having
ordered his little pages, in private, to goad on the dromedaries,
loud fits of laughter broke forth from the cages; for, the unwieldy
curvetting* of these poor beasts, and the ridiculous distress of their
superannuated riders, afforded the ladies no small entertainment.

---

*Leaping on hind legs.

They descended, however, unhurt into the valley, by the easy slopes which the emir had ordered to be cut in the rock; and already, the murmuring of streams and the rustling of leaves began to catch their attention. The cavalcade soon entered a path, which was skirted by flowering shrubs, and extended to a vast wood of palm trees, whose branches overspread a vast building of free stone. This edifice was crowned with nine domes, and adorned with as many portals of bronze, on which was engraven the following inscription: "This is the asylum of pilgrims, the refuge of travellers, and the depositary of secrets from all parts of the world."

Nine pages, beautiful as the day, and decently clothed in robes of Egyptian linen, were standing at each door. They received the whole retinue with an easy and inviting air. Four of the most amiable placed the Caliph on a magnificent tecthtrevan[57]: four others, somewhat less graceful, took charge of Bababalouk, who capered for joy at the snug little cabin that fell to his share; the pages that remained waited on the rest of the train.

Every man being gone out of sight, the gate of a large inclosure, on the right, turned on its harmonious hinges; and a young female, of a slender form, came forth. Her light brown hair floated in the hazy breeze of the twilight. A troop of young maidens, like the Pleiades, attended her on tip-toe. They hastened to the pavilions that contained the sultanas: and the young lady, gracefully bending, said to them: "Charming princesses, every thing is ready: we have prepared beds for your repose, and strewed your apartments with jasmine: no insects will keep off slumber from visiting your eye-lids; we will dispel them with a thousand plumes. Come then, amiable ladies, refresh your delicate feet, and your ivory limbs, in baths of rose water[58]; and, by the light of perfumed lamps, your servants will amuse you with tales." The sultanas accepted, with pleasure, these obliging offers; and followed the young lady to the emir's harem; where we must, for a moment, leave them, and return to the Caliph.

Vathek found himself beneath a vast dome, illuminated by a thousand lamps of rock crystal: as many vases of the same material, filled with excellent sherbet, sparkled on a large table, where a profusion of viands were spread. Amongst others, were rice boiled in milk of almonds, saffron soups, and lamb à la crême[59]; of all which the Caliph was amazingly fond. He took of each, as much as he was able, testified his sense of the emir's friendship, by the gaiety of his heart; and made the dwarfs dance, against their will[60]: for these little devotees durst not refuse[61] the commander of the faithful. At last, he spread himself on the sopha, and slept sounder than he ever had before.

Beneath this dome, a general silence prevailed; for there was nothing to disturb it but the jaws of Bababalouk, who had untrussed himself to eat with greater advantage; being anxious to make amends for his fast, in the mountains. As his spirits were too high to admit of his sleeping; and hating to be idle, he proposed with himself to visit the harem and repair to his charge of the ladies: to examine if they had been properly lubricated with the balm of Mecca[62]; if their eye-brows, and tresses, were in order; and, in a word, to perform all the little offices they might need. He sought for a long time together but without being able to find out the door. He durst not speak aloud for fear of disturbing the Caliph; and not a soul was stirring in the precincts of the palace. He almost despaired of effecting his purpose, when a low whispering just reached his ear. It came from the dwarfs, who were returned to their old occupation, and, for the nine hundred and ninety-ninth time in their lives, were reading over the Koran. They very politely invited Bababalouk to be of their party; but his head was full of other concerns. The dwarfs, though not a little scandalized at his dissolute morals, directed him to the apartments he wanted to find. His way thither lay through a hundred dark corridors, along which he groped as he went; and at last, began to catch, from the extremity of a passage, the charming gossiping of the women which not a little delighted his heart. "Ah, ha! what not yet asleep?" cried he; and, taking long strides as he spoke, "did you not suspect me of abjuring my charge?" Two of the black eunuchs, on hearing a voice so loud, left their party in haste, sabre in hand[63], to discover the cause: but, presently, was repeated on all sides: "'Tis only Bababalouk! no one but Bababalouk!" This circumspect guardian, having gone up to a thin veil of carnation-colour silk that hung before the door-way, distinguished, by means of the softened splendor that shone through it, an oval bath of dark porphyry surrounded by curtains, festooned in large folds. Through the apertures between them, as they were not drawn close, groups of young slaves were visible; amongst whom, Bababalouk perceived his pupils, indulgingly expanding their arms, as if to embrace the perfumed water, and refresh themselves after their fatigues. The looks of tender languor; their confidential whispers; and the enchanting smiles with which they were imparted; the exquisite fragrance of the roses: all combined to inspire a voluptuousness, which even Bababalouk himself was scarce able to withstand.

He summoned up, however, his usual solemnity, and in the peremptory tone of authority, commanded the ladies, instantly, to leave the bath. Whilst he was issuing these mandates, the young Nouronihar, daughter of the emir, who was as sprightly as an antelope, and full of wanton gaiety, beckoned one of her slaves to let down the great swing[64] which was suspended to the ceiling by cords of silk: and whilst this was doing, winked to her companions in the bath: who, chagrined to be forced from so soothing a state of indolence, began to twist and entangle their hair to plague and detain Bababalouk; and teased him besides with a thousand vagaries.

Nouronihar perceiving that he was nearly out of patience accosted him, with an arch air of respectful concern, and said: "My lord! it is not, by any means decent, that the chief eunuch of the Caliph our sovereign should thus continue standing: deign but to recline your graceful person upon this sofa which will burst with vexation, if it have not the honour to receive you." Caught by these flattering accents, Bababalouk gallantly replied: "Delight of the apple of my eye! I accept the invitation of your honied lips; and, to say truth, my senses are dazzled with the radiance that beams from your charms."—"Repose, then, at your ease," replied the beauty; as she placed him on the pretended sofa which, quicker than lightning, flew up all at once. The rest of the women, having aptly conceived her design, sprang naked from the bath, and plied the swing, with such unmerciful jerks, that it swept through the whole compass of a very lofty dome, and took from the poor victim all power of respiration. Sometimes, his feet rased the surface of the water; and, at others, the skylight almost flattened his nose. In vain did he fill the air with the cries of a voice that resembled the ringing of a cracked jar; their peals of laughter were still predominant.

Nouronihar, in the inebriety of youthful spirits, being used only to eunuchs of ordinary harems; and having never seen any thing so eminently disgusting, was far more diverted than all of the rest. She began to parody some Persian verses and sang with an accent most demurely piquant: "Oh gentle white dove, as thou soar'st through the air, vouchsafe one kind glance on the mate of thy love: melodious Philomel, I am thy rose[65]; warble some couplet to ravish my heart!"

The sultanas and their slaves, stimulated by these pleasant-ries, persevered at the swing, with such unremitted assiduity, that at length, the cord which had secured it, snapt suddenly asunder; and Bababalouk fell, floundering like a turtle, to the bottom of the bath. This accident occasioned an universal shout. Twelve little doors, till now unobserved, flew open at once; and the ladies, in an instant, made their escape; but not before having heaped all the towels on his head and put out the lights that remained.

The deplorable animal, in water to the chin, overwhelmed with darkness, and unable to extricate himself from the wrappers that embarrassed him, was still doomed to hear, for his further consolation, the fresh bursts of merriment his disaster occasioned. He bustled, but in vain, to get from the bath; for, the margin was become so slippery, with the oil spilt in breaking the lamps[66], that, at every effort, he slid back with a plunge which resounded aloud through the hollow of the dome. These cursed peals of laughter, were redoubled at every relapse, and he, who thought the place infested rather by devils than women, resolved to cease groping, and abide in the bath; where he amused himself with soliloquies, interspersed with imprecations, of which his malicious neighbours, reclining on down, suffered not an accent to escape. In this delectable plight, the morning surprised him. The Caliph, wondering at his absence, had caused him to be sought for every where. At last, he was drawn forth almost smothered from under the wisp of linen, and wet even to the marrow. Limping, and his teeth chattering with cold, he approached his master; who inquired what was the matter, and how he came soused in so strange a pickle?—"And why did you enter this cursed lodge?" answered Bababalouk, gruffly.—"Ought a monarch like you to visit with his harem, the abode of a grey-bearded emir, who knows nothing of life?— And, with what gracious damsels doth the place too abound! Fancy to yourself how they have soaked me like a burnt crust;

and made me dance like a jack-pudding,* the live-long night through, on their damnable swing. What an excellent lesson for your sultanas, into whom I had instilled such reserve and decorum!" Vathek, comprehending not a syllable of all this invective, obliged him to relate minutely the transaction: but, instead of sympathizing with the miserable sufferer, he laughed immoderately at the device of the swing and the figure of Bababalouk, mounted upon it. The stung eunuch could scarcely preserve the semblance of respect. "Aye, laugh, my lord! laugh," said he; "but I wish this Nouronihar would play some trick on you; she is too wicked to spare even majesty itself." These words made, for the present, but a slight impression on the Caliph; but they, not long after, recurred to his mind.

This conversation was cut short by Fakreddin, who came to request that Vathek would join in the prayers and ablutions, to be solemnized on a spacious meadow watered by innumerable streams. The Caliph found the waters refreshing, but the prayers abominably irksome. He diverted himself, however, with the multitude of calenders[67], santons[68], and derviches[69], who were continually coming and going; but especially with the bramins[70], faquirs[71], and other enthusiasts, who had travelled from the heart of India, and halted on their way with the emir. These latter had each of them some mummery peculiar to himself. One dragged a huge chain wherever he went; another an ouran-outang; whilst a third, was furnished with scourges; and all performed to a charm. Some would climb up trees, holding one foot in the air; others poise themselves over a fire, and, without mercy, fillip their noses. There were some amongst them that cherished vermin[72], which were not ungrateful in requiting their caresses. These rambling fanatics revolted the hearts of the

---

*A buffoon character, a staple of street performers.

derviches, the calenders, and santons; however, the vehemence of their aversion soon subsided, under the hope that the presence of the Caliph would cure their folly, and convert them to the mussulman faith. But, alas! how great was their disappointment! for Vathek, instead of preaching to them, treated them as buffoons, bade them present his compliments to Visnow and Ixhora[73], and discovered a predilection for a squat old man from the Isle of Serendib, who was more ridiculous than any of the rest. "Come!" said he, "for the love of your gods, bestow a few slaps on your chops to amuse me." The old fellow, offended at such an address, began loudly to weep; but, as he betrayed a villainous drivelling in shedding tears, the Caliph turned his back and listened to Bababalouk, who whispered, whilst he held the umbrella over him: "Your majesty should be cautious of this odd assembly; which hath been collected, I know not for what. Is it necessary to exhibit such spectacles to a mighty potentate, with interludes of talapoins[74] more mangy than dogs? Were I you, I would command a fire to be kindled, and at once rid the estates of the emir, of his harem, and all his menagerie."—"Tush, dolt," answered Vathek; "and know, that all this infinitely charms me. Nor shall I leave the meadow, till I have visited every hive of these pious mendicants."

Wherever the Caliph directed his course, objects of pity were sure to swarm round him[75]; the blind, the purblind, smarts without noses, damsels without ears, each to extol the munificence of Fakreddin, who, as well as his attendant grey-beards, dealt about, gratis, plasters and cataplasms* to all that applied. At noon, a superb corps of cripples made its appearance; and soon after advanced, by platoons, on the plain, the completest association of invalids that had ever been embodied till then.

---

*Plasters or poultices—medical treatments.

The blind went groping with the blind, the lame limped on together, and the maimed made gestures to each other with the only arm that remained. The sides of a considerable water-fall were crowded by the deaf; amongst whom were some from Pegû, with ears uncommonly handsome and large, but who were still less able to hear than the rest. Nor were there wanting others in abundance with hump-backs; wenny necks; and even horns of an exquisite polish.

The emir, to aggrandize the solemnity of the festival, in honour of his illustrious visitant, ordered the turf to be spread, on all sides, with skins and table-cloths; upon which were served up for the good Mussulmans, pilaus of every hue, with other orthodox dishes; and, by the express order of Vathek, who was shamefully tolerant, small plates of abominations[76] were prepared, to the great scandal of the faithful. The holy assembly began to fall to. The Caliph, in spite of every remonstrance from the chief of his eunuchs, resolved to have a dinner dressed on the spot. The complaisant emir immediately gave orders for a table to be placed in the shade of the willows. The first service consisted of fish, which they drew from a river, flowing over sands of gold at the foot of a lofty hill. These were broiled as fast as taken, and served up with a sauce of vinegar, and small herbs that grew on mount Sinai[77]: for every thing with the emir was excellent and pious.

The dessert was not quite set on, when the sound of lutes, from the hill, was repeated by the echoes of the neighbouring mountains. The Caliph, with an emotion of pleasure and surprize, had no sooner raised up his head, than a handful of jasmine dropped on his face. An abundance of tittering succeeded the frolic, and instantly appeared, through the bushes, the elegant forms of several young females, skipping and bounding like roes. The fragrance diffused from their hair, struck the sense of Vathek, who, in an ecstacy, suspending his repast, said to Bababalouk: "Are the peries[78] come down from their spheres? Note her, in particular, whose form is so perfect; venturously running on the brink of the precipice, and turning back her head, as regardless of nothing but the graceful flow of her robe. With what captivating impatience doth she contend with the bushes for her veil? could it be her who threw the jasmine at me!"—"Aye! she it was; and you too would she throw, from the top of the rock," answered Bababalouk; "for that is my good friend Nouronihar, who so kindly lent me her swing. My dear lord and master," added he, wresting a twig from a willow, "let me correct her for her want of respect: the emir will have no reason to complain; since (bating what I owe to his piety) he is much to be blamed for keeping a troop of girls on the mountains, where the sharpness of the air gives their blood too brisk a circulation."

"Peace! blasphemer," said the Caliph; "speak not thus of her, who, over these mountains, leads my heart a willing captive. Contrive, rather, that my eyes may be fixed upon her's: that I may respire her sweet breath as she bounds panting along these delightful wilds!" On saying these words, Vathek extended his arms towards the hill, and directing his eyes, with an anxiety unknown to him before, endeavoured to keep within view the object that enthralled his soul: but her course was as difficult to follow, as the flight of one of those beautiful blue butterflies of Cachemire[79], which are, at once, so volatile and rare.

The Caliph, not satisfied with seeing, wished also to hear Nouronihar, and eagerly turned to catch the sound of her voice. At last, he distinguished her whispering to one of her companions behind the thicket from whence she had thrown the jasmine: "A Caliph, it must be owned, is a fine thing to see; but my little Gulchenrouz is much more amiable: one lock of his hair is of more value to me than the richest embroidery of the Indies. I had rather that his teeth should mischievously press my finger, than the richest ring of the imperial treasure. Where have you left him, Sutlememe? and why is he not here?"

The agitated Caliph still wished to hear more; but she immediately retired with all her attendants. The fond monarch pursued her with his eyes till she was gone out of sight; and then continued like a bewildered and benighted traveller, from whom the clouds had obscured the constellation that guided his way. The curtain of night seemed dropped before him: every thing appeared discoloured. The falling waters filled his soul with dejection, and his tears trickled down the jasmines he had caught from Nouronihar, and placed in his inflamed bosom. He snatched up a few shining pebbles, to remind him of the scene where he felt the first tumults of love. Two hours were elapsed, and evening drew on, before he could resolve to depart from the place. He often, but in vain, attempted to go: a soft languor enervated the powers of his mind. Extending himself on the brink of the stream, he turned his eyes towards the blue summits of the mountain, and exclaimed, "What concealest thou behind thee, pitiless rock? what is passing in thy solitudes? Whither is she gone? O heaven! perhaps she is now wandering in thy grottoes with her happy Gulchenrouz!"

In the mean time, the damps began to descend; and the emir, solicitous for the health of the Caliph, ordered the imperial litter to be brought. Vathek, absorbed in his reveries, was imperceptibly removed and conveyed back to the saloon, that received him the evening before. But, let us leave the Caliph immersed in his new passion: and attend Nouronihar beyond the rocks where she had again joined her beloved Gulchenrouz.

This Gulchenrouz was the son of Ali Hassan, brother to the emir: and the most delicate and lovely creature in the

world. Ali Hassan, who had been absent ten years, on a voyage to the unknown seas, committed, at his departure, this
child, the only survivor of many, to the care and protection
of his brother. Gulchenrouz could write in various characters with precision, and paint upon vellum the most elegant
arabesques that fancy could devise. His sweet voice accompanied the lute in the most enchanting manner; and, when
he sang the loves of Megnoun and Leilah[80], or some unfortunate lovers of ancient days, tears insensibly overflowed
the cheeks of his auditors. The verses he composed (for, like
Megnoun, he, too, was a poet) inspired that unresisting languor, so frequently fatal to the female heart. The women all
doated upon him; and, though he had passed his thirteenth
year, they still detained him in the harem. His dancing was
light as the gossamer waved by the zephyrs of spring; but his
arms, which twined so gracefully with those of the young
girls in the dance, could neither dart the lance in the chace[81],
nor curb the steeds that pastured in his uncle's domains. The
bow, however, he drew with a certain aim, and would have
excelled his competitors in the race, could he have broken the
ties that bound him to Nouronihar.

The two brothers had mutually engaged their children to
each other[82]; and Nouronihar loved her cousin, more than her
own beautiful eyes[83]. Both had the same tastes and amusements;
the same long, languishing looks[84]; the same tresses; the same
fair complexions; and, when Gulchenrouz appeared in the dress
of his cousin, he seemed to be more feminine than even herself.
If, at any time, he left the harem, to visit Fakreddin; it was with
all the bashfulness of a fawn, that consciously ventures from the
lair of its dam: he was, however, wanton enough to mock the
solemn old grey-beards, though sure to be rated without mercy
in return. Whenever this happened, he would hastily plunge

into the recesses of the harem; and, sobbing, take refuge in the fond arms of Nouronihar who loved even his faults beyond the virtues of others.

It fell out this evening, that, after leaving the Caliph in the meadow, she ran with Gulchenrouz over the green sward of the mountain, that sheltered the vale where Fakreddin had chosen to reside. The sun was dilated on the edge of the horizon; and the young people, whose fancies were lively and inventive, imagined they beheld, in the gorgeous clouds of the west, the domes of Shaddukian and Ambreabad[85], where the Peries have fixed their abode. Nouronihar, sitting on the slope of the hill, supported on her knees the perfumed head of Gulchenrouz. The unexpected arrival of the Caliph and the splendour that marked his appearance, had already filled with emotion the ardent soul of Nouronihar. Her vanity irresistibly prompted her to pique the prince's attention; and this, she before took good care to effect, whilst he picked up the jasmine she had thrown upon him. But, when Gulchenrouz asked after the flowers he had culled for her bosom, Nouronihar was all in confusion. She hastily kissed his forehead; arose in a flutter; and walked, with unequal steps, on the border of the precipice. Night advanced, and the pure gold of the setting sun had yielded to a sanguine red; the glow of which, like the reflection of a burning furnace, flushed Nouronihar's animated countenance. Gulchenrouz, alarmed at the agitation of his cousin, said to her, with a supplicating accent—"Let us begone; the sky looks portentous; the tamarisks tremble more than common; and the raw wind chills my very heart. Come! let us begone; 'tis a melancholy night!" Then, taking hold of her hand, he drew it towards the path he besought her to go. Nouronihar, unconsciously followed the attraction; for, a thousand strange imaginations occupied her spirits. She passed the large round of honey-suckles, her favourite resort, without ever vouchsafing it a glance; yet Gulchenrouz could not help snatching off a few shoots in his way, though he ran as if a wild beast were behind.

The young females seeing them approach in such haste, and, according to custom, expecting a dance, instantly assembled in a circle and took each other by the hand: but, Gulchenrouz coming up out of breath, fell down at once on the grass. This accident struck with consternation the whole of this frolicsome party; whilst Nouronihar, half distracted and overcome, both by the violence of her exercise, and the tumult of her thoughts, sunk feebly down at his side; cherished his cold hands in her bosom, and chafed his temples with a fragrant perfume. At length, he came to himself; and, wrapping up his head in the robe of his cousin, intreated that she would not return to the harem. He was afraid of being snapped at by Shaban his tutor; a wrinkled old eunuch of a surly disposition; for, having interrupted the wonted walk of Nouronihar, he dreaded lest the churl should take it amiss. The whole of this sprightly group, sitting round upon a mossy knoll, began to entertain themselves with various pastimes; whilst their superintendants, the eunuchs, were gravely conversing at a distance. The nurse of the emir's daughter, observing her pupil sit ruminating with her eyes on the ground, endeavoured to amuse her with diverting tales; to which Gulchenrouz, who had already forgotten his inquietudes, listened with a breathless attention. He laughed; he clapped his hands; and passed a hundred little tricks on the whole of the company, without omitting the eunuchs whom he provoked to run after him, in spite of their age and decrepitude.

During these occurrences, the moon arose, the wind subsided, and the evening became so serene and inviting, that a resolution was taken to sup on the spot. One of the eunuchs ran to fetch melons whilst others were employed in showering down almonds from the branches that overhung this amiable party. Sutlememe, who excelled in dressing a salad, having filled large bowls of porcelain with eggs of small birds, curds turned with citron juice, slices of cucumber, and the inmost leaves of delicate herbs, handed it round from one to another and gave each their shares with a large spoon of cocknos[86]. Gulchenrouz, nestling, as usual, in the bosom of Nouronihar, pouted out his vermillion little lips against the offer of Sutlememe; and would take it, only, from the hand of his cousin, on whose mouth he hung, like a bee inebriated with the nectar of flowers.

In the midst of this festive scene, there appeared a light on the top of the highest mountain, which attracted the notice of every eye. This light was not less bright than the moon when at full, and might have been taken for her, had not the moon already risen. The phenomenon occasioned a general surprize and no one could conjecture the cause. It could not be a fire, for the light was clear and bluish: nor had meteors ever been seen of that magnitude or splendour. This strange light faded, for a moment; and immediately renewed its brightness. It first appeared motionless, at the foot of the rock; whence it darted in an instant, to sparkle in a thicket of palm-trees: from thence it glided along the torrent; and at last fixed in a glen that was narrow and dark. The moment it had taken its direction, Gulchenrouz, whose heart always trembled at any thing sudden or rare, drew Nouronihar by the robe and anxiously requested her to return to the harem. The women were importunate in seconding the intreaty; but the curiosity of the emir's daughter prevailed. She not only refused to go back, but resolved, at all hazards, to pursue the appearance.

Whilst they were debating what was best to be done, the light shot forth so dazzling a blaze that they all fled away shrieking. Nouronihar followed them a few steps; but, coming to the turn of a little bye path, stopped, and went back alone. As she ran with an alertness peculiar to herself, it was not long before she came to the place, where they had just been supping. The globe of fire now appeared stationary in the glen, and burned in majestic stillness. Nouronihar, pressing her hands upon her bosom, hesitated, for some moments, to advance. The solitude of her situation was new; the silence of the night, awful; and every object inspired sensations, which, till then, she never had felt. The affright of Gulchenrouz recurred to her mind, and she, a thousand times turned to go back; but this luminous appearance was always before her. Urged on by an irresistible impulse, she continued to approach it, in defiance of every obstacle that opposed her progress.

At length she arrived at the opening of the glen; but, instead of coming up to the light, she found herself surrounded by darkness; excepting that, at a considerable distance, a faint spark glimmered by fits. She stopped, a second time: the sound of water-falls mingling their murmurs; the hollow rustlings among the palm-branches; and the funeral screams of the birds from their rifted trunks: all conspired to fill her soul with terror. She imagined, every moment, that she trod on some venomous reptile. All the stories of malignant Dives and dismal Goules[87] thronged into her memory: but, her curiosity was, notwithstanding, more predominant than her fears. She, therefore, firmly entered a winding track that led towards the spark; but, being a stranger to the path, she had not gone far, till she began to repent of her rashness. "Alas!" said she, "that I were but in those secure and illuminated apartments, where my evenings glided on with Gulchenrouz! Dear child! how would thy heart flutter with terror, wert thou wandering in these wild solitudes, like me!" Thus speaking, she advanced, and, coming up to steps hewn in the rock, ascended them undismayed. The light, which was now gradually enlarging, appeared above her on the summit of the mountain, and as if proceeding from a cavern. At length, she distinguished a plaintive and melodious union of voices, that resembled the dirges which are sung over tombs. A sound, like that which arises from the filling of baths, struck her ear at the same time. She continued ascending, and discovered large wax torches in full blaze, planted here and there in the fissures of the rock. This appearance filled her with fear, whilst the subtle and potent odour, which the torches exhaled, caused her to sink, almost lifeless, at the entrance of the grot.

Casting her eyes within, in this kind of trance, she beheld a large cistern of gold, filled with a water, the vapour of which distilled on her face a dew of the essence of roses. A soft symphony resounded through the grot. On the sides of the cistern, she noticed appendages of royalty, diadems and feathers of the heron, all sparkling with carbuncles[88]. Whilst her attention was fixed on this display of magnificence, the music ceased, and a voice instantly demanded: "For what monarch are these torches kindled, this bath prepared, and these habiliments which belong, not only to the sovereigns of the earth, but even to the talismanick powers!" To which a second voice answered: "They are for the charming daughter of the emir Fakreddin."—"What," replied the first, "for that trifler, who consumes her time with a giddy child, immersed in softness, and who, at best, can make but a pitiful husband?"—"And can she," rejoined the other voice, "be amused with such empty toys, whilst the Caliph, the sovereign of the world, he who is destined to enjoy the treasures of the preadamite sultans; a prince six feet high; and whose eyes pervade the inmost soul of a female, is inflamed with love for her. No! she will be wise enough to answer that passion alone, that can aggrandize her glory. No doubt she will; and despise the puppet of her fancy. Then all the riches this place contains, as well as the carbuncle of Giamschid[89], shall be her's."—"You judge right," returned the first voice; "and I haste to Istakhar, to prepare the palace of subterranean fire for the reception of the bridal pair."

The voices ceased; the torches were extinguished[90], the most entire darkness succeeded; and Nouronihar recovering, with a start, found herself reclined on a sofa, in the harem of her father. She clapped her hands[91], and immediately came together, Gulchenrouz and her women; who, in despair at having lost her, had dispatched eunuchs to seek her, in every direction. Shaban appeared with the rest, and began to reprimand her, with an air of consequence: "Little impertinent," said he, "have you false keys, or are you beloved of some Genius, that hath given you a picklock? I will try the extent of your power: come to the dark chamber, and expect not the company of Gulchenrouz:—be expeditious! I will shut you up, and turn the key twice upon you!" At these menaces, Nouronihar indignantly raised her head, opened on Shaban her black eyes, which, since the important dialogue of the enchanted grot, were considerably enlarged, and said: "Go, speak thus to slaves; but learn to reverence her who is born to give laws and subject all to her power."

Proceeding in the same style, she was interrupted by a sudden exclamation of, "The Caliph! the Caliph!" All the curtains were thrown open, the slaves prostrated themselves in double rows, and poor little Gulchenrouz went to hide beneath the couch of a sofa. At first appeared a file of black eunuchs trailing after them long trains of muslin embroidered with gold, and holding in their hands censers, which dispensed, as they passed, the grateful perfume of the wood of aloes. Next marched Bababalouk with a solemn strut, and tossing his head, as not overpleased at the visit. Vathek came close after, superbly robed: his gait was unembarrassed and noble; and his presence would have engaged admiration, though he had not been the sovereign of the world. He approached Nouronihar with a throbbing heart, and seemed enraptured at the full effulgence of her radiant eyes, of which he had before caught but a few glimpses: but she instantly depressed them, and her confusion augmented her beauty.

Bababalouk, who was a thorough adept in coincidences of this nature, and knew that the worst game should be played with the best face, immediately made a signal for all to retire; and no sooner did he perceive beneath the sofa the little one's feet, than he drew him forth without ceremony, set him upon his shoulders, and lavished on him, as he went off, a thousand unwelcome caresses. Gulchenrouz cried out, and resisted till his cheeks became the colour of the blossom of pomegranates, and his tearful eyes sparkled with indignation. He cast a signif- icant glance at Nouronihar, which the Caliph noticing, asked, "Is that, then, your Gulchenrouz?"—"Sovereign of the world!" answered she, "spare my cousin, whose innocence and gentle- ness deserve not your anger!"—"Take comfort," said Vathek, with a smile; "he is in good hands. Bababalouk is fond of chil- dren; and never goes without sweetmeats and comfits." The daughter of Fakreddin was abashed, and suffered Gulchenrouz to be borne away without adding a word. The tumult of her bosom betrayed her confusion, and Vathek becoming still more impassioned, gave a loose to his frenzy; which had only not subdued the last faint strugglings of reluctance, when the emir suddenly bursting in, threw his face upon the ground, at the feet of the Caliph, and said: "Commander of the faithful! abase not yourself to the meanness of your slave."—"No, emir," replied Vathek, "I raise her to an equality with myself: I declare her my wife; and the glory of your race shall extend from one generation to another."—"Alas! my lord," said Fakreddin, as he plucked off a few grey hairs of his beard; "cut short the days of your faithful servant, rather than force him to depart from his word. Nouronihar is solemnly promised to Gulchenrouz, the son of my brother Ali Hassan: they are united, also, in heart; their faith is mutually plighted; and affiances, so sacred, cannot be broken."—"What then!" replied the Caliph, bluntly, "would you surrender this divine beauty to a husband more womanish than herself; and can you imagine, that I will suffer her charms to decay in hands so inefficient and nerveless? No! she is destined to live out her life within my embraces: such is my will: retire; and disturb not the night I devote to the worship of her charms."

The irritated emir drew forth his sabre, presented it to Vathek, and, stretching out his neck, said, in a firm tone of voice: "Strike your unhappy host, my lord! he has lived long enough, since he hath seen the prophet's vicegerent violate the rights of hospitality." At his uttering these words, Nouronihar, unable to support any longer the conflict of her passions, sunk down in a swoon. Vathek, both terrified for her life, and furious at an opposition to his will, bade Fakreddin assist his daughter, and withdrew; darting his terrible look at the unfortunate emir, who suddenly fell backward, bathed in a sweat as cold as the damp of death.

Gulchenrouz, who had escaped from the hands of Bababalouk and was, that instant, returned, called out for help, as loudly as he could, not having strength to afford it himself. Pale and panting, the poor child attempted to revive Nouronihar by caresses; and it happened, that the thrilling warmth of his lips restored her to life. Fakreddin beginning also to recover from the look of the Caliph, with difficulty tottered to a seat; and, after warily casting round his eye, to see if this dangerous Prince were gone, sent for Shaban and Sutlememe; and said to them apart: "My friends! violent evils require violent remedies: the Caliph has brought desolation and horror into my family; and, how, shall we resist his power? Another of his looks will send me to the grave. Fetch, then, that narcotick powder which a dervish brought me from Aracan. A dose of it, the effect of which will continue three days, must be administered to each of these children. The Caliph will believe them to be dead; for, they will have all the appearance of death. We shall go, as if to inter them in the cave of Meimoune, at the entrance of the great desert of sand and near the bower of my dwarfs. When all the spectators shall be withdrawn, you, Shaban, and four select eunuchs, shall convey them to the lake; where provision shall be ready to support them a month: for, one day allotted to the surprize this event will occasion; five, to the tears; a fortnight to reflection; and the rest, to prepare for renewing his progress; will, according to my calculation, fill up the whole time that Vathek will tarry; and I shall, then, be freed from his intrusion."

"Your plan is good," said Sutlememe, "if it can but be effected. I have remarked, that Nouronihar is well able to support the glances of the Caliph: and, that he is far from being sparing of them to her: be assured, therefore, that withstanding her fondness for Gulchenrouz, she will never remain quiet, while she knows him to be here. Let us persuade her, that both herself and Gulchenrouz are really dead; and, that they were conveyed to those rocks, for a limited season, to expiate the little faults, of which their love was the cause. We will add, that we killed ourselves in despair; and that your dwarfs, whom they never yet saw, will preach to them delectable sermons. I will engage that every thing shall succeed to the bent of your wishes."—"Be it so!" said Fakreddin, "I approve your proposal: let us lose not a moment to give it effect."

They hastened to seek for the powder which, being mixed in a sherbet, was immediately administered to Gulchenrouz and Nouronihar. Within the space of an hour, both were seized with violent palpitations; and a general numbness gradually ensued.

They arose from the floor where they had remained ever since the Caliph's departure; and, ascending to the sofa, reclined themselves upon it, clasped in each other's embraces. "Cherish me, my dear Nouronihar!" said Gulchenrouz: "put thy hand upon my heart; it feels as if it were frozen. Alas! thou art as cold as myself! hath the Caliph murdered us both, with his terrible look?"—"I am dying!" cried she, in a faultering voice: "Press me closer; I am ready to expire!"—"Let us die then, together," answered the little Gulchenrouz; whilst his breast laboured with a convulsive sigh: "let me, at least, breathe forth my soul on thy lips!" They spoke no more, and became as dead.

Immediately, the most piercing cries were heard through the harem; whilst Shaban and Sutlememe personated with great adroitness, the parts of persons in despair. The emir, who was sufficiently mortified, to be forced into such untoward expedients; and had now, for the first time, made a trial of his powder, was under no necessity of counterfeiting grief. The slaves, who had flocked together from all quarters, stood motionless, at the spectacle before them. All lights were extinguished, save two lamps; which shed a wan glimmering over the faces of these lovely flowers that seemed to he faded in the springtime of life. Funeral vestments were prepared; their bodies were washed[92], with rose-water; their beautiful tresses were braided and incensed; and they were wrapped in symars* whiter than alabaster.

At the moment, that their attendants were placing two wreaths of their favourite jasmines, on their brows, the Caliph, who had just heard the tragical catastrophe, arrived. He looked not less pale and haggard than the goules that wander, at night, among the graves. Forgetful of himself and every one else, he

---

*Loose dresses or robes.

broke through the midst of the slaves; fell prostrate at the foot of the sofa; beat his bosom; called himself "atrocious murderer!" and invoked upon his head, a thousand imprecations. With a trembling hand he raised the veil that covered the countenance of Nouronihar, and uttering a loud shriek, fell lifeless on the floor. The chief of the eunuchs dragged him off, with horrible grimaces, and repeated as he went, "Aye, I foresaw she would play you some ungracious turn!"

No sooner was the Caliph gone, than the emir commanded biers to be brought, and forbad that any one should enter the harem. Every window was fastened; all instruments of music were broken[93]; and the Imans began to recite their prayers[94]. Towards the close of this melancholy day, Vathek sobbed in silence; for they had been forced to compose, with anodynes, his convulsions of rage and desperation.

At the dawn of the succeeding morning, the wide folding doors of the palace were set open, and the funeral procession moved forward for the mountain. The wailful cries of "La Ilah illa Alla!" reached the Caliph, who was eager to cicatrize[*] himself, and attend the ceremonial: nor could he have been dissuaded, had not his excessive weakness disabled him from walking. At the few first steps he fell on the ground, and his people were obliged to lay him on a bed, where he remained many days in such a state of insensibility as excited compassion in the emir himself.

When the procession was arrived at the grot of Meimoune, Shaban and Sutlememe dismissed the whole of the train, excepting the four confidential eunuchs who were appointed to remain. After resting some moments near the biers, which had been left in the open air; they caused them to be carried

---

*Literally, this means to heal with scabs. Presumably, here Beckford simply means that Vathek wishes to recover from his "convulsions" and unhappiness.

to the brink of a small lake, whose banks were overgrown with a hoary moss. This was the great resort of herons and storks which preyed continually on little blue fishes. The dwarfs, instructed by the emir, soon repaired thither; and, with the help of the eunuchs, began to construct cabins of rushes and reeds, a work in which they had admirable skill. A magazine also was contrived for provisions, with a small oratory for themselves, and a pyramid of wood, neatly piled to furnish the necessary fuel: for the air was bleak in the hollows of the mountains.

At evening two fires were kindled on the brink of the lake, and the two lovely bodies, taken from their biers, were carefully deposited upon a bed of dried leaves, within the same cabin. The dwarfs began to recite the Koran, with their clear, shrill voices; and Shaban and Sutlememe stood at some distance, anxiously waiting the effects of the powder. At length Nouronihar and Gulchenrouz faintly stretched out their arms; and, gradually opening their eyes, began to survey, with looks of increasing amazement, every object around them. They even attempted to rise; but, for want of strength, fell back again. Sutlememe, on this, administered a cordial, which the emir had taken care to provide.

Gulchenrouz, thoroughly aroused, sneezed out aloud: and, raising himself with an effort that expressed his surprize, left the cabin and inhaled the fresh air, with the greatest avidity. "Yes," said he, "I breathe again! again do I exist! I hear sounds! I behold a firmament, spangled over with stars!"—Nouronihar, catching these beloved accents, extricated herself from the leaves and ran to clasp Gulchenrouz to her bosom. The first objects she remarked, were their long simars, their garlands of flowers, and their naked feet: she hid her face in her hands to reflect. The vision of the enchanted bath, the despair of her father, and, more vividly than both, the majestic figure of Vathek, recurred to her memory. She recollected also, that herself and Gulchenrouz had been sick and dying; but all these images bewildered her mind. Not knowing where she was, she turned her eyes on all sides, as if to recognize the surrounding scene. This singular lake, those flames reflected from its glassy surface, the pale hues of its banks, the romantic cabins, the bullrushes, that sadly waved their drooping heads; the storks, whose melancholy cries blended with the shrill voices of the dwarfs, every thing conspired to persuade her, that the angel of death had opened the portal of some other world[95].

Gulchenrouz, on his part, lost in wonder, clung to the neck of his cousin. He believed himself in the region of phantoms; and was terrified at the silence she preserved. At length addressing her; "Speak," said he, "where are we? do you not see those spectres that are stirring the burning coals? Are they Monker and Nekir[96] who are come to throw us into them? Does the fatal bridge[97] cross this lake, whose solemn stillness, perhaps, conceals from us an abyss, in which, for whole ages, we shall be doomed incessantly to sink."

"No, my children," said Sutlememe, going towards thorn, "take comfort! the exterminating angel, who conducted our souls hither after yours, hath assured us, that the chastisement of your indolent and voluptuous life, shall be restricted to a certain series of years[98], which you must pass in this dreary abode; where the sun is scarcely visible, and where the soil yields neither fruits nor flowers. These," continued she, pointing to the dwarfs, "will provide for our wants; for souls, so mundane as ours, retain too strong a tincture of their earthly extraction. Instead of meats, your food will be nothing but rice; and your bread shall be moistened in the fogs that brood over the surface of the lake."

At this desolating prospect, the poor children burst into

tears, and prostrated themselves before the dwarfs; who perfectly supported their characters, and delivered an excellent
discourse, of a customary length, upon the sacred camel[99];
which, after a thousand years, was to convey them to the paradise of the faithful.

The sermon being ended, and ablutions performed, they
praised Alla and the Prophet; supped very indifferently; and
retired to their withered leaves. Nouronihar and her little cousin,
consoled themselves on finding that the dead might lay in one
cabin. Having slept well before, the remainder of the night was
spent in conversation on what had befallen them; and both,
from a dread of apparitions, betook themselves for protection
to one another's arms.

In the morning, which was lowering and rainy, the dwarfs
mounted high poles, like minarets, and called them to prayers.
The whole congregation, which consisted of Sutlememe,
Shaban, the four eunuchs, and a few storks that were tired of
fishing, was already assembled. The two children came forth
from their cabin with a slow and dejected pace. As their minds
were in a tender and melancholy mood, their devotions were
performed with fervour. No sooner were they finished than
Gulchenrouz demanded of Sutlememe, and the rest, "how they
happened to die so opportunely for his cousin and himself?"—
"We killed ourselves," returned Sutlememe, "in despair at your
death." On this, Nouronihar who, notwithstanding what had
past had not yet forgotten her vision said—"And the Caliph!
is he also dead of his grief? and will he likewise come hither?"
The dwarfs, who were prepared with an answer, most demurely
replied: "Vathek is damned beyond all redemption!"—"I readily believe so," said Gulchenrouz; "and am glad, from my heart,
to hear it; for I am convinced it was his horrible look that sent
us hither, to listen to sermons, and mess upon rice." One week

passed away, on the side of the lake, unmarked by any variety: Nouronihar ruminating on the grandeur of which death had deprived her; and Gulchenrouz applying to prayers and basket-making with the dwarfs, who infinitely pleased him.

Whilst this scene of innocence was exhibiting in the mountains, the Caliph presented himself to the emir in a new light[100]. The instant he recovered the use of his senses, with a voice that made Bababalouk quake, he thundered out: "Perfidious Giaour! I renounce thee for ever! it is thou who hast slain my beloved Nouronihar! and I supplicate the pardon of Mahomet; who would have preserved her to me, had I been more wise. Let water be brought, to perform my ablutions, and let the pious Fakreddin be called to offer up his prayers with mine, and reconcile me to him. Afterwards, we will go together and visit the sepulchre of the unfortunate Nouronihar. I am resolved to become a hermit, and consume the residue of my days on this mountain, in hope of expiating my crimes."—"And what do you intend to live upon there?" inquired Bababalouk: "I hardly know," replied Vathek, "but I will tell you when I feel hungry—which, I believe, will not soon he the case."

The arrival of Fakreddin put a stop to this conversation. As soon as Vathek saw him, he threw his arms around his neck, bedewed his face with a torrent of tears, and uttered things so affecting, so pious, that the emir, crying for joy, congratulated himself, in his heart upon having performed so admirable and unexpected a conversion. As for the pilgrimage to the mountain, Fakreddin had his reasons not to oppose it; therefore, each ascending his own litter, they started.

Notwithstanding the vigilance with which his attendants watched the Caliph, they could not prevent his harrowing his cheeks with a few scratches, when on the place where he was told Nouronihar had been buried; they were even obliged to drag him away, by force of hands, from the melancholy spot. However he swore, with a solemn oath, that he would return thither every day. This resolution did not exactly please the emir—yet he flattered himself that the Caliph might not proceed farther, and would merely perform his devotions in the cavern of Meimouné. Besides, the lake was so completely concealed within the solitary bosom of those tremendous rocks, that he thought it utterly impossible any one could ever find it. This security of Fakreddin was also considerably strengthened by the conduct of Vathek, who performed his vow most scrupulously, and returned daily from the hill so devout, and so contrite, that all the grey-beards were in a state of ecstasy on account of it.

Nouronihar was not altogether so content; for though she felt a fondness for Gulchenrouz, who, to augment the attachment, had been left at full liberty with her, yet she still regarded him as but a bauble that bore no competition with the carbuncle of Giamschid. At times, she indulged doubts on the mode of her being; and scarcely could believe that the dead had all the wants and the whims of the living. To gain satisfaction, however, on so perplexing a topic; one morning, whilst all were asleep, she arose with a breathless caution from the side of Gulchenrouz: and, after having given him a soft kiss, began to follow the windings of the lake, till it terminated with a rock, the top of which was accessible, though lofty. This she climbed with considerable toil; and, having reached the summit, set forward in a run, like a doe before the hunter. Though she skipped with the alertness of an antelope, yet, at intervals, she was forced to desist, and rest beneath the tamarisks to recover her breath. Whilst she, thus reclined, was occupied with her little reflections on the apprehension that she had some knowledge of the place; Vathek, who, finding himself that morning but ill at ease, had gone forth before the dawn, presented himself, on a sudden, to her view. Motionless with surprise, he durst not approach the figure before him trembling and pale, but yet lovely to behold. At length, Nouronihar, with a mixture of pleasure and affliction, raising her fine eyes to him, said: "My lord! are you then come hither to eat rice and hear sermons with me?"—"Beloved phantom!" cried Vathek, "thou dost speak; thou hast the same graceful form; the same radiant features: art thou palpable likewise?" and, eagerly embracing her, added: "Here are limbs and a bosom, animated with a gentle warmth!—What can such a prodigy mean?"

Nouronihar, with indifference answered: "You know, my lord, that I died on the very night you honoured me with your visit. My cousin maintains it was from one of your glances; but I cannot believe him: for, to me, they seem not so dreadful. Gulchenrouz died with me, and we were both brought into a region of desolation, where we are fed with a wretched diet. If you be dead also, and are come hither to join us, I pity your lot: for, you will be stunned with the clang of the dwarfs and the storks. Besides, it is mortifying in the extreme, that you, as well as myself, should have lost the treasures of the subterranean palace."

At the mention of the subterranean palace, the Caliph suspended his caresses, (which indeed had proceeded pretty far) to seek from Nouronihar an explanation of her meaning. She then recapitulated her vision; what immediately followed; and the history of her pretended death; adding, also, a description of the place of expiation, from whence she had fled; and all, in a manner, that would have extorted his laughter, had not the thoughts of Vathek been too deeply engaged. No sooner, however, had she ended, than he again clasped her to his bosom and said: "Light of my eyes! the mystery is unravelled; we both are alive! Your father is a cheat, who, for the sake of dividing us, hath deluded us both: and the Giaour, whose design, as far as I can discover, is, that we shall proceed together, seems scarce a whit better. It shall be some time, at least, before he finds us in his palace of fire. Your lovely little person, in my estimation, is far more precious than all the treasures of the pre-adamite sultans; and I wish to possess it at pleasure, and, in open day, for many a moon, before I go to burrow under ground, like a mole. Forget this little trifler, Gulchenrouz; and"—"Ah! my lord!" interposed Nouronihar, "let me intreat that you do him no evil."—"No, no!" replied Vathek, "I have already bid you forbear to alarm yourself for him. He has been brought up too much on milk and sugar to stimulate my jealousy. We will leave him with the dwarfs; who, by the bye, are my old acquaintances: their company will suit him far better than yours. As to other matters; I will return no more to your father's. I want not to have my ears dinned by him and his dotards with the violation of the rights of hospitality: as if it were less an honour for you to espouse the sovereign of the world, than a girl dressed up like a boy!"

Nouronihar could find nothing to oppose, in a discourse so eloquent. She only wished the amorous monarch had discovered more ardour for the carbuncle of Giamschid: but flattered herself it would gradually increase; and, therefore, yielded to his will, with the most bewitching submission.

When the Caliph judged it proper, he called for Bababalouk, who was asleep in the cave of Meimouné, and dreaming that the phantom of Nouronihar, having mounted him once more on her swing, had just given him such a jerk, that he, one moment, soared above the mountains, and the next, sunk into the abyss. Starting from his sleep at the sound of his master, he ran, gasping for breath, and had nearly fallen backward at the sight, as he believed, of the spectre, by whom he had, so lately, been haunted in his dream. "Ah, my lord!" cried he, recoiling ten steps, and covering his eyes with both hands, "do you then perform the office of a goul! have you dug up the dead? yet hope not to make her your prey: for, after all she hath caused me to suffer, she is wicked enough to prey even upon you."

"Cease to play the fool," said Vathek, "and thou shalt soon be convinced that it is Nouronihar herself, alive and well, whom I clasp to my breast. Go and pitch my tents in the neighbouring valley. There will I fix my abode, with this beautiful tulip, whose colours I soon shall restore. There exert thy best endeavours to procure whatever can augment the enjoyments of life, till I shall disclose to thee more of my will."

The news of so unlucky an event soon reached the ears of the emir, who abandoned himself to grief and despair, and began, as did his old grey-beards, to begrime his visage with ashes. A total supineness ensued; travellers were no longer entertained; no more plasters were spread; and, instead of the charitable activity that had distinguished this asylum, the whole of its inhabitants exhibited only faces of half a cubit long, and uttered groans that accorded with their forlorn situation.

Though Fakreddin bewailed his daughter, as lost to him for ever, yet Gulchenrouz was not forgotten. He dispatched immediate instruction to Sutlememe, Shaban, and the dwarfs, enjoining them not to undeceive the child, in respect to his state; but, under some pretence, to convey him far from the lofty rock, at the extremity of the lake, to a place which he should appoint, as safer from danger, for he suspected that Vathek intended him evil.

Gulchenrouz, in the meanwhile, was filled with amazement, at not finding his cousin; nor were the dwarfs less surprised; but Sutlememe, who had more penetration, immediately guessed what had happened. Gulchenrouz was amused with the delusive hope of once more embracing Nouronihar, in the interior recesses of the mountains, where the ground, strewed over with orange blossoms and jasmines, offered beds much more inviting than the withered leaves in their cabin; where they might accompany, with their voices, the sounds of their lutes, and chase butterflies. Sutlememe was far gone in this sort of description, when one of the four eunuchs beckoned her aside, to apprize her of the arrival of a messenger from their fraternity, who had explained the secret of the flight of Nouronihar, and brought the commands of the emir. A council with Shaban and the dwarfs was immediately held. Their baggage being stowed in consequence of it, they embarked in a shallop,* and quietly sailed with the little one, who acquiesced in all their proposals. Their voyage proceeded in the same manner, till they came to the place where the lake sinks beneath the hollow of a rock; but, as soon as the bark had entered it and Gulchenrouz found himself surrounded with darkness, he was seized with a dreadful consternation, and incessantly uttered the most piercing outcries; for he now was persuaded he should actually be damned for having taken too many little freedoms, in his life-time, with his cousin.

But let us return to the Caliph, and her who ruled over his heart. Bababalouk had pitched the tents, and closed up the extremities of the valley, with magnificent screens of India cloth, which were guarded by Ethiopian slaves with their drawn sabres. To preserve the verdure of this beautiful inclosure in its natural freshness, white eunuchs went continually round it with gilt water vessels. The waving of fans was heard near the imperial pavilion; where, by the voluptuous light that glowed through the muslins, the Caliph enjoyed, at full view, all the

---

*Probably a light sailing vessel, though there were heavier shallops with masts as well.

attractions of Nouronihar. Inebriated with delight, he was all ear to her charming voice, which accompanied the lute: while she was not less captivated with his descriptions of Samarah, and the tower full of wonders; but especially with his relation of the adventure of the ball, and the chasm of the Giaour, with its ebony portal.

In this manner they conversed the whole day, and at night they bathed together, in a basin of black marble, which admirably set off the fairness of Nouronihar. Bababalouk, whose good graces this beauty had regained, spared no attention, that their repasts might be served up with the minutest exactness: some exquisite rarity was ever placed before them; and he sent even to Schiraz, for that fragrant and delicious wine, which had been hoarded up in bottles, prior to the birth of Mahomet[101]. He had excavated little ovens in the rock[102], to bake the nice manchets which were prepared by the hands of Nouronihar, from whence they had derived a flavour so grateful to Vathek, that he regarded the ragouts of his other wives as entirely maukish: whilst they would have died of chagrin at the emir's, at finding themselves so neglected, if Fakreddin, notwithstanding his resentment, had not taken pity upon them.

The sultana Dilara, who, till then, had been the favourite, took this dereliction of the Caliph to heart, with a vehemence natural to her character: for, during her continuance in favour, she had imbibed from Vathek many of his extravagant fancies, and was fired with impatience to behold the superb tombs of Istakar, and the palace of forty columns; besides, having been brought up amongst the magi, she had fondly cherished the idea of the Caliph's devoting himself to the worship of fire: thus, his voluptuous and desultory life with her rival, was to her a double source of affliction. The transient piety of Vathek had occasioned her some serious alarms; but the present was an evil of far greater magnitude. She resolved, therefore, without hesitation, to write to Carathis, and acquaint her that all things went ill; that they had eaten, slept, and revelled at an old emir's, whose sanctity was very formidable; and that, after all, the prospect of possessing the treasures of the pre-adamite sultans, was no less remote than before. This letter was entrusted to the care of two woodmen, who were at work in one of the great forests of the mountains; and who, being acquainted with the shortest cuts, arrived in ten days at Samarah.

The Princess Carathis was engaged at chess with Morakanabad, when the arrival of these wood-fellers was announced. She, after some weeks of Vathek's absence, had forsaken the upper regions of her tower, because every thing appeared in confusion among the stars, which she consulted, relative to the fate of her son. In vain did she renew her fumigations, and extend herself on the roof, to obtain mystic visions; nothing more could she see in her dreams, than pieces of brocade, nosegays of flowers, and other unmeaning gew-gaws. These disappointments had thrown her into a state of dejection, which no drug in her power was sufficient to remove. Her only resource was in Morakanabad, who was a good man, and endowed with a decent share of confidence; yet, whilst in her company, he never thought himself on roses.

No person knew aught of Vathek, and, of course, a thousand ridiculous stories were propagated at his expense. The eagerness of Carathis may be easily guessed at receiving the letter, as well as her rage at reading the dissolute conduct of her son. "Is it so!" said she: "either I will perish, or Vathek shall enter the palace of fire. Let me expire in flames, provided he may reign on the throne of Soliman!" Having said this, and whirled herself round in a magical manner, which struck Morakanabad with such terror as caused him to recoil, she ordered her great camel Alboufaki to be brought, and the hideous Nerkes, with the unrelenting Cafour, to attend. "I require no other retinue," said she to Morakanabad: "I am going on affairs of emergency; a truce, therefore, to parade! Take you care of the people; fleece them well in my absence, for we shall expend large sums, and one knows not what may betide."

The night was uncommonly dark, and a pestilential blast blew from the plain of Catoul, that would have deterred any other traveller however urgent the call: but Carathis enjoyed most whatever filled others with dread. Nerkes concurred in opinion with her; and Cafour had a particular predilection for a pestilence. In the morning this accomplished caravan, with the woodfellers, who directed their route, halted on the edge of an extensive marsh, from whence so noxious a vapour arose, as would have destroyed any animal but Alboufaki, who naturally inhaled these malignant fogs with delight. The peasants entreated their convoy not to sleep in this place. "To sleep," cried Carathis, "what an excellent thought! I never sleep, but for visions; and, as to my attendants, their occupations are too many, to close the only eye they have." The poor peasants, who were not over-pleased with their party, remained open-mouthed with surprise.

Carathis alighted, as well as her negresses; and, severally stripping off their outer garments, they all ran to cull from those spots, where the sun shone fiercest, the venomous plants that grew on the marsh. This provision was made for the family of the emir; and whoever might retard the expedition to Istakar. The woodmen were overcome with fear, when they beheld these three horrible phantoms run; and, not much relishing the company of Alboufaki, stood aghast at the command of Carathis to set forward; notwithstanding it was noon, and the heat fierce enough to calcine even rocks. In spite however, of every remonstrance, they were forced implicitly to submit.

Alboufaki, who delighted in solitude, constantly snorted whenever he perceived himself near a habitation; and Carathis, who was apt to spoil him with indulgence, as constantly turned him aside: so that the peasants were precluded from procuring subsistence; for, the milch goats and ewes, which Providence had sent towards the district they traversed to refresh travellers with their milk, all fled at the sight of the hideous animal and his strange riders. As to Carathis, she needed no common aliment; for, her invention had previously furnished her with an opiate, to stay her stomach; some of which she imparted to her mutes.

At dusk, Alboufaki making a sudden stop, stampt with his foot; which, to Carathis, who knew his ways, was a certain indication that she was near the confines of some cemetery[103]. The moon shed a bright light on the spot, which served to discover a long wall with a large door in it, standing a-jar; and so high that Alboufaki might easily enter. The miserable guides, who perceived their end approaching, humbly implored Carathis, as she had now so good an opportunity, to inter them; and immediately gave up the ghost. Nerkes and Cafour, whose wit was of a style peculiar to themselves, were by no means parsimonious of it on the folly of these poor people; nor could any thing have been found more suited to their taste, than the site of the burying ground, and the sepulchres which its precincts contained. There were, at least, two thousand of them on the declivity of a hill. Carathis was too eager to execute her plan, to stop at the view, charming as it appeared in her eyes. Pondering the advantages that might accrue from her present situation, she said to herself, "So beautiful a cemetery must be haunted by gouls! they never want for intelligence: having heedlessly suffered my stupid guides to expire, I will apply for directions to them; and, as an inducement, will invite them to regale on these fresh corpses." After this wise soliloquy, she beckoned to Nerkes and

Cafour, and made signs with her fingers, as much as to say: "Go; knock against the sides of the tombs and strike up your delightful warblings."

The negresses, full of joy at the behests of their mistress; and promising themselves much pleasure from the society of the gouls, went, with an air of conquest, and began their knockings at the tombs. As their strokes were repeated, a hollow noise was heard in the earth; the surface hove up into heaps; and the gouls, on all sides, protruded their noses to inhale the effluvia, which the carcases of the woodmen began to emit. They assembled before a sarcophagus of white marble, where Carathis was seated between the bodies of her miserable guides. The Princess received her visitants with distinguished politeness; and, supper being ended, they talked of business. Carathis soon learnt from them every thing she wanted to discover; and, without loss of time, prepared to set forward on her journey. Her negresses, who were forming tender connexions with the gouls, importuned her, with all their fingers, to wait at least till the dawn. But Carathis, being chastity in the abstract, and an implacable enemy to love intrigues and sloth, at once rejected their prayer; mounted Alboufaki, and commanded them to take their seats instantly. Four days and four nights, she continued her route without interruption. On the fifth, she traversed craggy mountains, and half-burnt forests; and arrived on the sixth, before the beautiful screens which concealed from all eyes the voluptuous wanderings of her son.

It was day-break, and the guards were snoring on their posts in careless security, when the rough trot of Alboufaki awoke them in consternation. Imagining that a group of spectres, ascended from the abyss, was approaching, they all, without ceremony, took to their heels. Vathek was, at that instant, with Nouronihar in the bath; hearing tales, and laughing at Bababalouk, who related them: but, no sooner did the outcry of his guards reach him, than he flounced from the water like a carp; and as soon threw himself back at the sight of Carathis; who, advancing with her negresses, upon Alboufaki, broke through the muslin awnings and veils of the pavilion. At this sudden apparition, Nouronihar (for she was not, at all times, free from remorse) fancied, that the moment of celestial vengeance was come; and clung about the Caliph, in amorous despondence.

Carathis, still seated on her camel, foamed with indignation, at the spectacle which obtruded itself on her chaste view. She thundered forth without check or mercy: "Thou double-headed and four-legged monster! what means all this winding and writhing? art them not ashamed to be seen grasping this limber sapling; in preference to the sceptre of the pre-adamite sultans? Is it then, for this paltry doxy, that thou hast violated the conditions in the parchment of our Giaour! Is it on her, thou hast lavished thy precious moments! Is this the fruit of the knowledge I have taught thee! Is this the end of thy journey? Tear thyself from the arms of this little simpleton; drown her, in the water before me; and, instantly follow my guidance."

In the first ebullition of his fury, Vathek had resolved to rip open the body of Alboufaki and to stuff it with those of the negresses and of Carathis herself, but the remembrance of the Giaour, the palace of Istakar, the sabres, and the talismans, flashing before his imagination, with the simultaneousness of lightning, he became more moderate, and said to his mother, in a civil, but decisive tone; "Dread lady! you shall be obeyed; but I will not drown Nouronihar. She is sweeter to me than a Myrabolan comfit[104]; and is enamoured of carbuncles; especially that, of Giamschid; which hath also been promised to be conferred upon her: she, therefore, shall go along with us; for, I intend to repose with her upon the sofas of Soliman: I can sleep no more without her."—"Be it so!" replied Carathis, alighting; and, at the same time, committing Alboufaki to the charge of her black women.

Nouronihar, who had not yet quitted her hold, began to take courage; and said, with an accent of fondness, to the Caliph: "Dear sovereign of my soul! I will follow thee, if it be thy will, beyond the Kaf, in the land of the afrits. I will not hesitate to climb, for thee, the nest of the Simurgh; who, this lady excepted, is the most awful of created beings."—"We have here then," subjoined Carathis, "a girl, both of courage and science!" Nouronihar had certainly both; but, notwithstanding all her firmness, she could not help casting back a thought of regret upon the graces of her little Gulchenrouz; and the days of tender endearments she had participated with him. She, even, dropped a few tears; which, the Caliph observed; and inadvertently breathed out with a sigh: "Alas! my gentle cousin! what will become of thee!"—Vathek, at this apostrophe, knitted up his brows; and Carathis inquired what it could mean? "She is preposterously sighing after a stripling with languishing eyes and soft hair, who loves her," said the Caliph. "Where is he?" asked Carathis. "I must be acquainted with this pretty child: for," added she, lowering her voice, "I design, before I depart, to regain the favour of the Giaour. There is nothing so delicious, in his estimation, as the heart of a delicate boy palpitating with the first tumults of love."

Vathek, as he came from the bath, commanded Bababalouk to collect the women, and other moveables of his harem; embody his troops; and hold himself in readiness to march within three days: whilst Carathis, retired alone to a tent, where the Giaour solaced her with encouraging visions: but, at length, waking, she found at her feet, Nerkes and Cafour, who informed her, by their signs, that having led Alboufaki to the borders of a lake;

to browse on some grey moss, that looked tolerably venomous; they had discovered certain blue fishes[105], of the same kind with those in the reservoir on the top of the tower. "Ah! ha!" said she, "I will go thither to them. These fish are past doubt of a species that, by a small operation, I can render oracular. They may tell me, where this little Gulchenrouz is; whom I am bent upon sacrificing." Having thus spoken, she immediately set out, with her swarthy retinue.

It being but seldom that time is lost, in the accomplishment of a wicked enterprize, Carathis and her negresses soon arrived at the lake; where, after burning the magical drugs, with which they were always provided; they stripped themselves naked, and waded to their chins; Nerkes and Cafour waving torches around them, and Carathis pronouncing her barbarous incantations. The fishes, with one accord, thrust forth their heads from the water; which was violently rippled by the flutter of their fins: and, at length, finding themselves constrained, by the potency of the charm, they opened their piteous mouths, and said: "From gills to tail, we are yours; what seek ye to know?"— "Fishes," answered she, "I conjure you, by your glittering scales; tell me where now is Gulchenrouz?"—"Beyond the rock," replied the shoal, in full chorus: "will this content you? for we do not delight in expanding our mouths."—"It will," returned the Princess: "I am not to learn, that you are not used to long conversations: I will leave you therefore to repose, though I had other questions to propound." The instant she had spoken, the water became smooth; and the fishes, at once, disappeared.

Carathis, inflated with the venom of her projects, strode hastily over the rock; and found the amiable Gulchenrouz, asleep, in an arbour; whilst the two dwarfs were watching at his side, and ruminating their accustomed prayers. These diminutive personages possessed the gift of divining, whenever an enemy to good

Mussulmans approached: thus, they anticipated the arrival of Carathis; who, stopping short, said to herself: "How placidly doth he recline his lovely little head! how pale, and languishing, are his looks! it is just the very child of my wishes!" The dwarfs interrupted this delectable soliloquy, by leaping, instantly, upon her; and scratching her face, with their utmost zeal. But Nerkes and Cafour, betaking themselves to the succour of their mistress, pinched the dwarfs so severely, in return, that they both gave up the ghost; imploring Mahomet to inflict his sorest vengeance upon this wicked woman, and all her household.

At the noise which this strange conflict occasioned in the valley, Gulchenrouz awoke; and, bewildered with terror, sprung impetuously and climbed an old fig-tree that rose against the acclivity of the rocks; from thence he gained their summits, and ran for two hours without once looking back. At last, exhausted with fatigue, he fell senseless into the arms of a good old Genius,* whose fondness for the company of children, had made it his sole occupation to protect them. Whilst performing his wonted rounds through the air, he had pounced on the cruel Giaour, at the instant of his growling in the horrible chasm, and had rescued the fifty little victims which the impiety of Vathek had devoted to his voracity. These the Genius brought up in nests still higher than the clouds, and himself fixed his abode, in a nest more capacious than the rest, from which he had expelled the Rocs that had built it.

These inviolable asylums were defended against the dives and the afrits, by waving streamers; on which were inscribed in characters of gold, that flashed like lightning, the names of Alla and the Prophet. It was there that Gulchenrouz, who, as yet remained undeceived with respect to his pretended death,

---

*That is to say, a Genii.

thought himself in the mansions of eternal peace. He admitted without fear the congratulations of his little friends, who were all assembled in the nest of the venerable Genius, and vied with each other in kissing his serene forehead and beautiful eye-lids.—Remote from the inquietudes of the world; the impertinence of harems, the brutality of eunuchs, and the inconstancy of women; there he found a place truly congenial to the delights of his soul. In this peaceable society his days, months, and years glided on; nor was he less happy than the rest of his companions: for the Genius, instead of burthening his pupils with perishable riches and vain sciences, conferred upon them the boon of perpetual childhood.

Carathis, unaccustomed to the loss of her prey, vented a thousand execrations on her negresses, for not seizing the child, instead of amusing themselves with pinching to death two insignificant dwarfs from which they gain no advantage. She returned into the valley murmuring; and, finding that her son was not risen from the arms of Nouronihar, discharged her ill-humour upon both. The idea, however, of departing next day for Istakar, and of cultivating, through the good offices of the Giaour, an intimacy with Eblis himself, at length consoled her chagrin. But fate had ordained it otherwise.

In the evening as Carathis was conversing with Dilara, who, through her contrivance had become of the party, and whose taste resembled her own, Bababalouk came to acquaint her that the sky towards Samarah looked of a fiery red, and seemed to portend some alarming disaster. Immediately recurring to her astrolabes[106] and instruments of magic, she took the altitude of the planets, and discovered, by her calculations, to her great mortification, that a formidable revolt had taken place at Samarah, that Motavakel, availing himself of the disgust, which was inveterate against his brother, had incited commotions amongst the populace, made himself master of the palace, and actually invested the great tower, to which Morakanabad had retired, with a handful of the few that still remained faithful to Vathek.

"What!" exclaimed she; "must I lose, then, my tower! my mutes! my negresses! my mummies! and, worse than all, the laboratory, the favourite resort of my nightly lucubrations, without knowing, at least, if my hair-brained son will complete his adventure? No! I will not be dupe! immediately will I speed to support Morakanabad. By my formidable art, the clouds shall pour grape-shot in the faces of the assailants and shafts of red-hot iron on their heads. I will let loose my stores of hungry serpents and torpedos, from beneath them; and we shall soon see the stand they will make against such an explosion!"

Having thus spoken, Carathis hasted to her son who was tranquilly banqueting with Nouronihar, in his superb carnation-coloured tent. "Glutton, that thou art!" cried she, "were it not for me, thou wouldst soon find thyself the mere commander of savoury pies. Thy faithful subjects have abjured the faith they swore to thee. Motavakel, thy brother, now reigns on the hill of Pied Horses: and, had I not some slight resources in the tower, would not be easily persuaded to abdicate. But, that time may not be lost, I shall only add a few words:—Strike tent to-night; set forward; and beware how thou loiterest again by the way. Though, thou hast forfeited the conditions of the parchment, I am not yet without hope: for, it cannot be denied, that thou hast violated, to admiration, the laws of hospitality by seducing the daughter of the emir, after having partaken of his bread and his salt. Such a conduct cannot but be delightful to the Giaour; and if, on thy march, thou canst signalize thyself, by an additional crime; all will still go well, and thou shalt enter the palace of Soliman, in triumph. Adieu! Alboufaki and my negresses are waiting at the door."

The Caliph had nothing to offer in reply: he wished his mother a prosperous journey, and ate on till he had finished his supper. At midnight, the camp broke up, amidst the flourishing of trumpets and other martial instruments; but loud indeed must have been the sound of the tymbals, to overpower the blubbering of the emir, and his grey-beards; who, by an excessive profusion of tears, had so far exhausted the radical moisture, that their eyes shrivelled up in their sockets, and their hairs dropped off by the roots. Nouronihar, to whom such a symphony was painful, did not grieve to get out of hearing. She accompanied the Caliph in the imperial litter; where they amused themselves, with imagining the splendour which was soon to surround them. The other women, overcome with dejection, were dolefully rocked in their cages; whilst Dilara consoled herself, with anticipating the joy of celebrating the rites of fire, on the stately terraces of Istakar.

In four days, they reached the spacious valley of Rocnabad. The season of spring was in all its vigour, and the grotesque branches of the almond trees, in full blossom, fantastically chequered with hyacinths and jonquils, breathed forth a delightful fragrance. Myriads of bees, and scarce fewer of santons,* had there taken up their abode. On the banks of the stream, hives and oratories[107] were alternately ranged; and their neatness and whiteness were set off, by the deep green of the cypresses, that spired up amongst them. These pious personages amused themselves, with cultivating little gardens, that abounded with flowers and fruits; especially, musk-melons, of the best flavour that Persia could boast. Sometimes dispersed over the meadow, they entertained themselves with feeding peacocks, whiter than snow; and turtles, more blue than the sapphire. In this manner were they occupied, when

---

*Monks or hermits.

the harbingers of the imperial procession began to proclaim: "Inhabitants of Rocnabad! prostrate yourselves on the brink of your pure waters; and tender your thanksgivings to heaven, that vouchsafeth to shew you a ray of its glory: for, lo! the commander of the faithful draws near."

The poor santons, filled with holy energy, having bustled to light up wax torches in their oratories, and expand the Koran on their ebony desks, went forth to meet the Caliph with baskets of honeycomb, dates, and melons. But, whilst they were advancing in solemn procession and with measured steps, the horses, camels, and guards, wantoned over their tulips and other flowers, and made a terrible havoc amongst them. The santons could not help casting from one eye a look of pity on the ravages committing around them; whilst, the other was fixed upon the Caliph and heaven. Nouronihar, enraptured with the scenery of a place which brought back to her remembrance the pleasing solitudes where her infancy had passed, intreated Vathek to stop: but he, suspecting that these oratories might be deemed, by the Giaour, an habitation, commanded his pioneers to level them all. The santons stood motionless with horror, at the barbarous mandate; and, at last, broke out into lamentations; but these were uttered with so ill a grace, that Vathek bade his eunuchs to kick them from his presence. He then descended from the litter, with Nouronihar. They sauntered together in the meadow; and amused themselves with culling flowers, and passing a thousand pleasantries on each other. But the bees, who were staunch Mussulmans, thinking it their duty to revenge the insult offered to their dear masters, the santons, assembled so zealously to do it with good effect, that the Caliph and Nouronihar were glad to find their tents prepared to receive them.

Bababalouk, who, in capacity of purveyor, had acquitted himself with applause, as to peacocks and turtles; lost no time in consigning some dozens to the spit; and as many more to be fricasseed. Whilst they were feasting, laughing, carousing, and blaspheming at pleasure, on the banquet so liberally furnished; the moullahs, the sheiks, the cadis[108], and imans of Schiraz (who seemed not to have met the santons) arrived; leading by bridles of riband, inscribed from the Koran, a train of asses[109] which were loaded with the choicest fruits the country could boast. Having presented their offerings to the Caliph; they petitioned him, to honour their city and mosques, with his presence. "Fancy not," said Vathek, "that you can detain me. Your presents I condescend to accept; but beg you will let me quiet; for, I am not over-fond of resisting temptation. Retire then:—Yet, as it is not decent, for personages so reverend, to return on foot; and, as you have not the appearance of expert riders, my eunuchs shall tie you on your asses with the precaution that your backs be not turned towards me: for, they understand etiquette."—In this deputation, were some high-stomached sheiks who, taking Vathek for a fool, scrupled not to speak their opinion. These, Bababalouk girded with double cords; and having well disciplined their asses with nettles behind, they all started, with a preternatural alertness; plunging, kicking, and running foul of one another, in the most ludicrous manner imaginable.

Nouronihar and the Caliph mutually contended who should most enjoy so degrading a sight. They burst out in peals of laughter, to see the old men and their asses fall into the stream. The leg of one was fractured; the shoulder of another, dislocated; the teeth of a third, dashed out; and the rest suffered still worse.

Two days more, undisturbed by fresh embassies, having been devoted to the pleasures of Rocnabad, the expedition proceeded; leaving Schiraz on the right, and verging towards a large plain; from whence were discernible, on the edge of the horizon, the dark summits of the mountains of Istakar.

At this prospect, the Caliph and Nouronihar were unable to repress their transports. They bounded from their litter to the ground; and broke forth into such wild exclamations, as amazed all within hearing. Interrogating each other, they shouted, "Are we not approaching the radiant palace of light? or gardens, more delightful than those of Sheddad?"—Infatuated mortals! they thus indulged delusive conjecture, unable to fathom the decrees of the Most High!

The good Genii, who had not totally relinquished the super-intendence of Vathek; repairing to Mahomet, in the seventh heaven; said: "Merciful Prophet! stretch forth thy propitious arms, towards thy vicegerent; who is ready to fall, irretrievably, into the snare, which his enemies, the dives, have prepared to destroy him. The Giaour is awaiting his arrival, in the abomina-ble palace of fire; where, if he once set his foot, his perdition will be inevitable." Mahomet answered, with an air of indignation: "He hath too well deserved to be resigned to himself; but I per-mit you to try if one effort more will be effectual to divert him from pursuing his ruin."

One of these beneficent Genii, assuming, without delay, the exterior of a shepherd, more renowned for his piety than all the derviches and santons of the region, took his station near a flock of white sheep, On the slope of a hill; and began to pour forth, from his flute, such airs of pathetic melody, as subdued the very soul; and, wakening remorse, drove, far from it, every frivolous fancy. At these energetic sounds, the sun hid himself beneath a gloomy cloud; and the waters of two little lakes, that were nat-urally clearer than crystal, became of a colour like blood. The whole of this superb assembly was involuntarily drawn towards the declivity of the hill. With downcast eyes, they all stood abashed; each upbraiding himself with the evil he had done. The heart of Dilara palpitated; and the chief of the eunuchs, with a sigh of contrition, implored pardon of the women, whom, for his own satisfaction, he had so often tormented.

Vathek and Nouronihar turned pale in their litter; and, regarding each other with haggard looks, reproached themselves—the one with a thousand of the blackest crimes; a thousand projects of impious ambition;—the other, with the desolation of her family; and the perdition of the amiable Gulchenrouz. Nouronihar persuaded herself that she heard, in the fatal music, the groans of her dying father; and Vathek, the sobs of the fifty children he had sacrificed to the Giaour. Amidst these complicated pangs of anguish, they perceived themselves impelled towards the shepherd, whose countenance was so commanding that Vathek, for the first time, felt overawed; whilst Nouronihar concealed her face with her hands. The music paused; and the Genius, addressing the Caliph, said: "Deluded prince! to whom Providence hath confided the care of innumerable subjects; is it thus that thou fulfillest thy mission? Thy crimes are already completed; and, art thou now hastening towards thy punishment? Thou knowest that, beyond these mountains, Eblis[110] and his accursed dives hold their infernal empire; and seduced by a malignant phantom, thou art proceeding to surrender thyself to them! This moment is the last of grace allowed thee: abandon thy atrocious purpose: return: give back Nouronihar to her father, who still retains a few sparks of life: destroy thy tower, with all its abominations: drive Carathis from thy councils: be just to thy subjects: respect the ministers of the Prophet; compensate for thy impieties, by an exemplary life[111]: and, instead of squandering thy days in voluptuous indulgence, lament thy crimes on the sepulchres of thy ancestors. Thou beholdest the clouds that obscure the sun: at the instant he recovers his splendour, if thy heart be not changed, the time of mercy assigned thee will be past for ever."

Vathek, depressed with fear, was on the point of prostrating himself at the feet of the shepherd; whom he perceived to be of a nature superior to man: but, his pride prevailing, he audaciously lifted his head, and, glancing at him one of his terrible looks, said: "Whoever thou art, withhold thy useless admonitions: thou wouldst either delude me, or art thyself deceived. If what I have done be so criminal, as thou pretendest, there remains not for me a moment of grace. I have traversed a sea of blood, to acquire a power, which will make thy equals tremble: deem not that I shall retire, when in view of the port; or, that I will relinquish her, who is dearer to me than either my life, or thy mercy. Let the sun appear! let him illume my career! it matters not where it may end." On uttering these words, which made even the Genius shudder, Vathek threw himself into the arms of Nouronihar; and commanded that his horses should be forced back to the road.

There was no difficulty in obeying these orders: for, the attraction had ceased: the sun shone forth in all his glory, and the shepherd vanished with a lamentable scream.

The fatal impression of the music of the Genius, remained, notwithstanding, in the heart of Vathek's attendants. They viewed each other with looks of consternation. At the approach of night, almost all of them escaped; and, of this numerous assemblage, there only remained the chief of the eunuchs, some idolatrous slaves, Dilara, and a few other women; who, like herself, were votaries of the religion of the Magi.

The Caliph, fired with the ambition of prescribing laws to the powers of darkness, was but little embarrassed at this dereliction. The impetuosity of his blood prevented him from sleeping; nor did he encamp any more, as before. Nouronihar, whose impatience, if possible exceeded his own, importuned him to hasten his march, and lavished on him a thousand caresses, to beguile all reflection. She fancied herself already more potent than Balkis[112], and pictured to her imagination the Genii falling prostrate at the foot of her throne. In this manner they advanced by moon-light, till they came within view of the two towering rocks that form a kind of portal to the valley, at the extremity of which, rose the vast ruins of Istakar. Aloft, on the mountain, glimmered the fronts of various royal mausoleums, the horror of which was deepened by the shadows of night. They passed through two villages, almost deserted; the only inhabitants remaining being a few feeble old men: who, at the sight of horses and litters, fell upon their knees, and cried out: "O Heaven! is it then by these phantoms that we have been, for six months tormented! Alas! it was from the terror of these spectres and the noise beneath the mountains, that our people have fled, and left us at the mercy of the malificent spirits!" The Caliph, to whom these complaints were but unpromising auguries, drove over the bodies of these wretched old men; and, at length, arrived at the foot of the terrace of black marble. There he descended from his litter, handing down Nouronihar; both with beating hearts, stared wildly around them, and expected, with an apprehensive shudder, the approach of the Giaour. But nothing as yet announced his appearance.

A death-like stillness reigned over the mountain and through the air. The moon dilated on a vast platform, the shades of the lofty columns which reached from the terrace almost to the clouds. The gloomy watch-towers, whose number could not be counted, were covered by no roof; and their capitals, of an architecture unknown in the records of the earth, served as an asylum for the birds of night, which, alarmed at the approach of such visitants, fled away croaking.

The chief of the eunuchs, trembling with fear, besought Vathek that a fire might be kindled. "No!" replied he, "there is no time left to think of such trifles; abide where thou art, and expect my commands." Having thus spoken, he presented his hand to Nouronihar; and, ascending the steps of a vast staircase, reached the terrace, which was flagged with squares of marble, and resembled a smooth expanse of water, upon whose surface not a blade of grass ever dared to vegetate. On the right rose the watch-towers, ranged before the ruins of an immense palace, whose walls were embossed with various figures. In front stood forth the colossal forms of four creatures, composed of the leopard and the griffin, and though but of stone, inspired emotions of terror. Near these were distinguished by the splendour of the moon, which streamed full on the place, characters like those on the sabres of the Giaour, and which possessed the same virtue of changing every moment. These, after vacillating for some time, fixed at last in Arabic letters, and prescribed to the Caliph the following words:—"Vathek! thou hast violated the conditions of my parchment, and deserveth to be sent back, but in favour to thy companion, and, as the meed for what thou hast done to obtain it; Eblis permitteth that the portal of his palace shall be opened; and the subterranean fire will receive thee into the number of its adorers."

He scarcely had read these words, before the mountain, against which the terrace was reared, trembled; and the watch-towers were ready to topple headlong upon them. The rock yawned, and disclosed within it a staircase of polished marble, that seemed to approach the abyss. Upon each stair were planted two large torches, like those Nouronihar had seen in her vision; the camphorated vapour of which ascended and gathered itself into a cloud under the hollow of the vault.

This appearance, instead of terrifying, gave new courage to the daughter of Fakreddin. Scarcely deigning to bid adieu to the moon, and the firmament; she abandoned, without hesitation, the pure atmosphere, to plunge into these infernal exhalations. The gait of those impious personages was haughty, and determined. As they descended, by the effulgence of the torches, they gazed on each other with mutual admiration; and both appeared so resplendent, that they already esteemed themselves spiritual intelligences. The only circumstance that perplexed them, was their not arriving at the bottom of the stairs. On hastening their descent, with an ardent impetuosity, they felt their steps accelerated to such a degree, that they seemed not walking but falling from a precipice. Their progress, however, was at length impeded, by a vast portal of ebony which the Caliph, without difficulty, recognized. Here, the Giaour awaited them, with the key in his hand. "Ye are welcome!" said he to them, with a ghastly smile, "in spite of Mahomet, and all his dependents. I will now usher you into that palace, where you have so highly merited a place." Whilst he was uttering these words, he touched the enameled lock with his key; and the doors, at once, flew open with a noise still louder than the thunder of the dog days, and as suddenly recoiled, the moment they had entered.

The Caliph and Nouronihar beheld each other with amazement, at finding themselves in a place, which, though roofed with a vaulted ceiling, was so spacious and lofty, that, at first, they took it for an immeasurable plain. But their eyes, at length, growing familiar to the grandeur of the surrounding objects, they extended their view to those at a distance; and discovered rows of columns and arcades, which gradually diminished, till they terminated in a point radiant as the sun, when he darts his last beams athwart the ocean. The pavement, strewed over with gold dust and saffron, exhaled so subtile an odour, as almost overpowered them. They, however, went on; and observed an infinity of censers, in which, ambergrise and the wood of aloes, were continually burning. Between the several columns, were placed tables; each, spread with a profusion of viands; and wines, of every species, sparkling in vases of crystal. A throng of Genii, and other fantastic spirits, of either sex, danced lasciviously, at the sound of music, which issued from beneath.

In the midst of this immense hall, a vast multitude was incessantly passing; who severally kept their right hands on their hearts; without once regarding any thing around them. They had all, the livid paleness of death. Their eyes, deep sunk in their sockets, resembled those phosphoric meteors, that glimmer by night, in places of interment. Some stalked slowly on; absorbed in profound reverie: some shrieking with agony, ran furiously about like tigers, wounded with poisoned arrows; whilst others, grinding their teeth in rage, foamed along more frantic than the wildest maniac. They all avoided each other; and, though surrounded by a multitude that no one could number, each wandered at random, unheedful of the rest, as if alone on a desert where no foot had trodden.

Vathek and Nouronihar, frozen with terror, at a sight so baleful, demanded of the Giaour what these appearances might mean; and, why these ambulating spectres never withdrew their hands from their hearts? "Perplex not yourselves, with so much at once," replied he bluntly; "you will soon be acquainted with all: let us haste, and present you to Eblis." They continued their way, through the multitude; but, notwithstanding their confidence at first, they were not sufficiently composed to examine, with attention, the various perspective of halls and of galleries, that opened on the right hand and left; which were all illuminated by torches and braziers, whose flames rose in pyramids to the centre of the vault. At length they came to a place, where long curtains brocaded with crimson and gold, fell from all parts in solemn confusion. Here, the choirs and dances were heard no longer. The light which glimmered, came from afar.

After some time, Vathek and Nouronihar perceived a gleam brightening through the drapery, and entered a vast tabernacle hung around with the skins of leopards. An infinity of elders with streaming beards, and afrits in complete armour, had prostrated themselves before the ascent of a lofty eminence; on the top of which, upon a globe of fire, sat the formidable Eblis. His person was that of a young man, whose noble and regular features seemed to have been tarnished by malignant vapours. In his large eyes appeared both pride and despair: his flowing hair retained some resemblance to that of an angel of light. In his hand, which thunder had blasted, he swayed the iron sceptre, that causes the monster Ouranbad[113], the afrits, and all the powers of the abyss to tremble. At his presence, the heart of the Caliph sunk within him; and he fell prostrate on his face. Nouronihar, however, though greatly dismayed, could not help admiring the person of Eblis: for, she expected to have seen some stupendous giant. Eblis, with a voice more mild than might be imagined, but such as penetrated the soul and filled it with the deepest melancholy, said: "Creatures of clay[114], I receive you into mine empire: ye are numbered amongst my adorers: enjoy whatever this palace affords: the treasures of the pre-adamite sultans; their fulminating sabres; and those talismans, that compel the dives to open the subterranean expanses of the mountain of Kaf, which communicate with these. There, insatiable as your curiosity may be, shall you find sufficient objects to gratify it. You shall possess the exclusive privilege of entering the fortresses of Aherman[115], and the halls of Argenk[116], where are pourtrayed all creatures endowed with intelligence; and the various animals that inhabited the earth prior to the creation of that contemptible being whom ye denominate the father of mankind."

Vathek and Nouronihar feeling themselves revived and encouraged by this harangue, eagerly said to the Giaour;

"Bring us instantly to the place which contains these precious talismans."—"Come," answered this wicked dive, with his malignant grin, "come and possess all that my sovereign hath promised; and more." He then conducted them into a long aisle adjoining the tabernacle; preceding them with hasty steps, and followed by his disciples with the utmost alacrity. They reached, at length, a hall of great extent, and covered with a lofty dome; around which appeared fifty portals of bronze, secured with as many fastenings of iron. A funeral gloom prevailed over the whole scene. Here, upon two beds of incorruptible cedar, lay recumbent the fleshless forms of the pre-adamite kings, who had been monarchs of the whole earth. They still possessed enough of life to be conscious of their deplorable condition. Their eyes retained a melancholy motion: they regarded one another with looks of the deepest dejection; each holding his right hand, motionless, on his heart[117]. At their feet were inscribed the events of their several reigns, their power, their pride, and their crimes; Soliman Daki; and Soliman, called Gian Ben Gian, who, after having chained up the dives in the dark caverns of Kaf, became so presumptuous as to doubt of the Supreme Power. All these maintained great state; though not to be compared with the eminence of Soliman Ben Daoud.

This king, so renowned for his wisdom, was on the loftiest elevation; and placed immediately under the dome. He appeared to possess more animation than the rest. Though, from time to time, he laboured with profound sighs; and, like his companions, kept his right hand on his heart; yet his countenance was more composed, and he seemed to be listening to the sullen roar of a cataract visible in part through one of the grated portals. This was the only sound that intruded on the silence of these doleful mansions. A range of brazen vases surrounded the elevation. "Remove the covers from these cabalistic depositaries," said the Giaour to Vathek; "and avail thyself of the talismans which will break asunder all these gates of bronze; and not only render thee master of the treasures contained within them, but also of the spirits by which they are guarded."

The Caliph, whom this ominous preliminary had entirely disconcerted, approached the vases with faltering footsteps; and was ready to sink with terror when he heard the groans of Soliman. As he proceeded, a voice from the livid lips of the prophet articulated these words: "In my life-time[118], I filled a magnificent throne; having, on my right hand, twelve thousand seats of gold, where the patriarchs and the prophets heard my doctrines; on my left, the sages and doctors, upon as many thrones of silver, were present at all my decisions. Whilst I thus administered justice to innumerable multitudes, the birds of the air, hovering over me, served as a canopy against the rays of the sun. My people flourished; and my palace rose to the clouds. I erected a temple to the Most High, which was the wonder of the universe: but, I basely suffered myself to be seduced by the love of women, and a curiosity that could not be restrained by sublunary things. I listened to the counsels of Aherman, and the daughter of Pharaoh; and adored fire, and the hosts of heaven. I forsook the holy city, and commanded the Genii to rear the stupendous palace of Istakar, and the terrace of the watch towers; each of which was consecrated to a star. There, for a while, I enjoyed myself in the zenith of glory and pleasure. Not only men, but supernatural beings were subject also to my will. I began to think, as these unhappy monarchs around had already thought, that the vengeance of Heaven was asleep; when, at once, the thunder burst my structures asunder, and precipitated me hither: where, however, I do not remain, like the other inhabitants, totally destitute of hope; for, an angel of light hath revealed that in consideration of the piety of my early youth, my woes shall come to an end, when this cataract shall for ever cease to flow. Till then I am in torments, ineffable torments! an unrelenting fire preys on my heart."

Having uttered this exclamation, Soliman raised his hands towards heaven, in token of supplication; and the Caliph discerned through his bosom, which was transparent as crystal, his heart enveloped in flames. At a sight so full of horror, Nouronihar fell back, like one petrified, into the arms of Vathek, who cried out with a convulsive sob; "O Giaour! whither hast thou brought us! Allow us to depart, and I will relinquish all thou hast promised. O Muhomet! remains there no more mercy!"—"None! none!" replied the malicious dive. "Know, miserable prince! thou art now in the abode of vengeance and despair. Thy heart, also, will be kindled like those of the other votaries of Eblis. A few days are allotted thee previous to this fatal period: employ them as thou wilt; recline on these heaps of gold; command the infernal potentates; range, at thy pleasure, through these immense subterranean domains: no barrier shall be shut against thee. As for me, I have fulfilled my mission: I now leave thee to thyself." At these words he vanished.

The Caliph and Nouronihar remained in the most abject affliction. Their tears were unable to flow, and scarcely could they support themselves. At length, taking each other, despondingly, by the hand, they went faltering from this fatal hall; indifferent which way they turned their steps. Every portal opened at their approach. The dives fell prostrate before them. Every reservoir of riches was disclosed to their view: but they no longer felt the incentives of curiosity, of pride, or avarice. With like apathy they heard the chorus of Genii, and saw the stately banquets prepared to regale them. They went wandering on, from chamber to chamber; hall to hall; and gallery to gallery; all without bounds or limit; all distinguishable by the same louring gloom; all adorned with the same awful grandeur; all traversed by persons in search of repose and consolation; but, who sought them in vain; for every one carried within him a heart tormented in flames. Shunned by these various sufferers, who seemed by their looks to be upbraiding the partners of their guilt, they withdrew from them to wait, in direful suspense, the moment which should render them to each other the like objects of terror.

"What!" exclaimed Nouronihar; "will the time come when I shall snatch my hand from thine!"—"Ah!" said Vathek, "and shall my eyes ever cease to drink from thine long draughts of enjoyment! Shall the moments of our reciprocal ecstasies be reflected on with horror! It was not thou that broughtest me hither; the principles by which Carathis perverted my youth, have been the sole cause of my perdition! it is but right she should have her share of it." Having given vent to these painful expressions, he called to an afrit, who was stirring up one of the braziers, and bade him fetch the Princess Carathis from the palace of Samarah.

After issuing these orders, the Caliph and Nouronihar continued walking amidst the silent croud, till they heard voices at the end of the gallery. Presuming them to proceed from some unhappy beings, who, like themselves, were awaiting their final doom; they followed the sound, and found it to come from a small square chamber, where they discovered, sitting on sofas, four young men, of goodly figure, and a lovely female, who were holding a melancholy conversation by the glimmering of a lonely lamp. Each had a gloomy and forlorn air; and two of them were embracing each other with great tenderness. On seeing the Caliph and the daughter of Fakreddin enter, they arose, saluted, and made room for them. Then he who appeared the most considerable of the group, addressed himself thus to

Vathek:—"Strangers! who doubtless are in the same state of suspense with ourselves, as you do not yet bear your hand on your heart, if you are come hither to pass the interval allotted, previous to the infliction of our common punishment, condescend to relate the adventures that have brought you to this fatal place; and we, in return, will acquaint you with ours, which deserve but too well to be heard. To trace back our crimes to their source, though we are not permitted to repent, is the only employment suited to wretches like us!"

The Caliph and Nouronihar assented to the proposal; and Vathek began, not without tears and lamentations, a sincere recital of every circumstance that had passed. When the afflicting narrative was closed, the young man, who first addressed him, began in the following manner:—"The history of the princes and friends, Alasi and Firouz, confined in the palace of subterraneous fire." The next was:—"The history of Prince Barkiarokh, confined in the palace of subterraneous fire." Then: "The history of Prince Kalilah and Princess Zulkais, confined in the palace of subterraneous fire." The third prince had reached the midst of his adventures, when a sudden noise interrupted him, which caused the vault to tremble and to open.

Immediately a cloud descended, which gradually dissipating, discovered Carathis on the back of an afrit[119], who grievously complained of his burden. She, instantly springing to the ground, advanced towards her son, and said, "What dost thou here, in this little square chamber? As the dives are become subject to thy beck, I expected to have found thee on the throne of the pre-adamite kings."

"Execrable woman!" answered the Caliph; "cursed be the day thou gavest me birth! Go, follow this afrit; let him conduct thee to the hall of the Prophet Soliman: there thou wilt learn to what these palaces are destined, and how much I ought to abhor the impious knowledge thou hast taught me."

"Has the height of power, to which thou art arrived, turned thy brain?" answered Carathis: "but I ask no more than permission to shew my respect for Soliman the prophet. It is, however, proper thou shouldest know that (as the afrit has informed me neither of us shall return to Samarah) I requested his permission to arrange my affairs; and he politely consented. Availing myself, therefore, of the few moments allowed me, I set fire to the tower, and consumed in it the mutes, negresses, and serpents, which have rendered me so much good service: nor should I have been less kind to Morakanabad, had he not prevented me, by deserting at last to thy brother. As for Bababalouk, who had the folly to return to Samarah, to provide husbands for thy wives, I undoubtedly would have put him to the torture; but being in a hurry, I only hung him, after having decoyed him in a snare, with thy wives: whom I buried alive by the help of my negresses; who thus spent their last moments greatly to their satisfaction. With respect to Dilara, who ever stood high in my favour, she hath evinced the greatness of her mind, by fixing herself near, in the service of one of the magi; and, I think, will soon be one of our society."

Vathek, too much cast down to express the indignation excited by such a discourse, ordered the afrit to remove Carathis from his presence, and continued immersed in thoughts which his companions durst not disturb.

Carathis, however, eagerly entered the dome of Soliman, and, without regarding in the least the groans of the prophet, undauntedly removed the covers of the vases, and violently seized on the talismans. Then, with a voice more loud than had hitherto been heard within these mansions, she compelled the dives to disclose to her the most secret treasures, the most profound stores, which the afrit himself had not seen. She passed, by rapid descents, known only to Eblis and his most favoured potentates; and thus penetrated the very entrails of the earth, where breathes the sansar, or the icy wind of death. Nothing appalled her dauntless soul. She perceived, however, in all the inmates who bore their hands on their heart, a little singularity, not much to her taste.

As she was emerging from one of the abysses, Eblis stood forth to her view; but, notwithstanding he displayed the full effulgence of his infernal majesty, she preserved her countenance unaltered; and even paid her compliments with considerable firmness.

This superb monarch thus answered: "Princess, whose knowledge, and whose crimes, have merited a conspicuous rank in my empire; thou dost well to avail yourself of the leisure that remains: for, the flames and torments, which are ready to seize on thy heart, will not fail to provide thee soon with full employment." He said, and was lost in the curtains of his tabernacle.

Carathis paused for a moment with surprise; but resolved to follow the advice of Eblis, she assembled all the choirs of genii, and all the dives, to pay her homage. Thus marched she, in triumph, through a vapour of perfumes, amidst the acclamations of all the malignant spirits; with most of whom she had formed a previous acquaintance. She even attempted to dethrone one of the Solimans, for the purpose of usurping his place; when a voice, proceeding from the abyss of death, proclaimed: "All is accomplished!" Instantaneously, the haughty forehead of the intrepid princess became corrugated with agony: she uttered a tremendous yell; and fixed, no more to be withdrawn, her right hand upon her heart, which was become a receptacle of eternal fire.

In this delirium, forgetting all ambitious projects, and her thirst for that knowledge which should ever be hidden from mortals, she overturned the offerings of the genii; and, having execrated the hour she was begotten and the womb that had borne her, glanced off in a rapid whirl that rendered her invisible[120], and continued to revolve without intermission.

Almost at the same instant, the same voice announced to the Caliph, Nouronihar, the four princes, and the princess, the awful, and irrevocable decree. Their hearts immediately took fire, and they, at once, lost the most precious gift of heaven:—HOPE[121]. These unhappy beings recoiled, with looks of the most furious distraction. Vathek beheld in the eyes of Nouronihar nothing but rage and vengeance; nor could she discern ought in his, but aversion and despair. The two princes who were friends, and, till that moment, had preserved their attachment, shrunk back, gnashing their teeth with mutual and unchangeable hatred. Kalilah and his sister made reciprocal gestures of imprecation; all testified their horror for each other by the most ghastly convulsions, and screams that could not be smothered. All severally plunged themselves into the accursed multitude, there to wander in an eternity of unabating anguish.

Such was, and such should be, the punishment of unrestrained passions and atrocious deeds! Such shall be, the chastisement of that blind curiosity, which would transgress those bounds the wisdom of the Creator has prescribed to human knowledge; and such the dreadful disappointment of that restless ambition, which, aiming at discoveries reserved for beings of a supernatural order, perceives not, through its infatuated pride, that the condition of man upon earth is to be humble and ignorant.

Thus the Caliph Vathek, who, for the sake of empty pomp and forbidden power, had sullied himself with a thousand crimes, became a prey to grief without end, and remorse without mitigation: whilst the humble, the despised Gulchenrouz passed whole ages in undisturbed tranquillity, and in the pure happiness of childhood.

NOTES

The following notes were added to Beckford's manuscript by the Rev. Samuel Henley (1740–1815) for the first edition of *Vathek* translated by Henley and published in England in 1786.

1 *Caliph*. This title amongst the Mahometans implies the three characters of Prophet, Priest, and King: it signifies, in the Arabic, *Successor*, or *Vicar*; and, by appropriation, the *Vicar of God on Earth*. It is, at this day, one of the titles of the Grand Signior, as successor of Mahomet; and of the Sophi of Persia, as successor of Ali. *Habesci's State of the Ottoman Empire*, p. 9. *D'Herbelot*, p. 985.

2 *one of his eyes became so terrible*. The author of *Nighiaristan* hath preserved a fact that supports this account; and there is no history of Vathek, in which his *terrible eye* is not mentioned.

3. *Omar Ben Abdalaziz*. This Caliph was eminent above all others for temperance and self-denial; insomuch, that, according to the Mahometan faith, he was raised to Mahomet's bosom, as a reward for his abstinence in an age of corruption. *D'Herbelot*, p. 690.

4. *Samarah*. A city of the Babylonian Irak; supposed to have stood on the site where Nimrod erected his tower. Khondemir relates, in his life of Motassem, that this prince, to terminate the disputes which were

perpetually happening between the inhabitants of Bagda and his Turkish slaves, withdrew from thence, and, having fixed on a situation in the plain of Catoul, there founded Samarah. He is said to have had in the stables of this city, a hundred and thirty thousand *pied horses*; each of which carried, by his order, a sack of earth to a place he had chosen. By this accumulation, an elevation was formed that commanded a view of all Samarah, and served for the foundation of his magnificent palace. *D'Herbelot*, p. 752. 808. 985. *Anecdotes Arabes*, p. 413.

5. *in the most delightful succession.* The great men of the East have been always fond of music. Though forbidden by the Mahometan religion, it commonly makes a part of every entertainment. *Nitimur in vetitum semper.* Female slaves are generally kept to amuse them, and the ladies of their harems.

6. *Mani.* This artist, whom Inatulla of Delhi styles *the far-famed*, lived in the reign of Schabur, or Sapor, the son of Ardschir Babegan; and was, by profession, a painter and sculptor. It appears, from the Arabian Nights, that Haroun al Raschid, Vathek's grandfather, had adorned his palace and furnished his magnificent pavilion, with the most capital performances of the Persian artists.

7. *Houris.* The virgins of Paradise, called, from their large black eyes, *Hur al oyun.* An intercourse with these, according to the institution of Mahomet, is to constitute the principal felicity of the faithful. Not formed of clay, like mortal women, they are adorned with unfading charms, and deemed to possess the celestial privilege of an eternal youth. *Al Koran; passim.*

8. *Mahomet in the seventh heaven.* In this heaven, the paradise of Mahomet is supposed to be placed contiguous to the throne of Alla. Hagi Khalfah relates, that Ben Iatmaiah, a celebrated doctor of Damascus, had the temerity to assert, that, when the Most High erected his throne, he reserved a vacant place for Mahomet upon it.

9. *Genii.* It is asserted, and not without plausible reasons, that the words *Genn, Ginn—Genius, Genie, Gian, Gigas, Giant, Geant* proceed from the same themes, *viz.* Γῆ, *the earth*, and Γάω *to produce;* as if these supernatural agents had been an early production of the earth, long before Adam was modelled

out from a lump of it. The Ὄντες and Εωντες of Plato, bear a close analogy to these supposed intermediate creatures between God and man. From these premises arose the consequence that, boasting a higher order, formed of more subtile matter and possessed of much greater knowledge than man, they lorded over this planet and invisibly governed it with superior intellect. From this last circumstance, they obtained in Greece, the title of Δαίμονες, Demons, from Δἀημων, *Sciens*, knowing. The Hebrew word סילפנ Nephilim. (Gen. Cap. vi. 4.) translated by *Gigantes*, giants, claiming the same etymon with Νεφελη a cloud, seems also to indicate that these intellectual beings inhabited the void expanse of the terrestrial atmosphere. Hence the very ancient fable of men of enormous strength and size revolting against the Gods, and all the mythological lore relating to that mighty conflict; unless we trace the origin of this important event to the ambition of Satan, his revolt against the Almighty and his fall with the angels.

10. *Assist him to complete the tower.* The genii were famous for their architectural skill. The pyramids of Egypt have been ascribed to Gian Ben Gian their chief, most likely, because they could not, from records, be attributed to any one else. According to the Koran, ch. 34, the genii were employed by Solomon in the erection of his temple. The reign of Gian Ben Gian, over the Peris, is said to have continued for two thousand years; after which, Eblis was sent by the Deity to exile them, on account of their disorders, and confine them in the remotest region of the earth. *D'Herbelot*, p. 396. *Bailly sur l'Atlantide*, p. 147.

11. *the stranger displayed such rarities as he had never before seen.* That such curiosities were much sought after in the days of Vathek, may be concluded from the encouragement which Haroun al Raschid gave to the mechanic arts, and the present he sent, by his ambassadors, to Charlemagne. This consisted of a clock, which, when put into motion, by means of a clepsydra, not only pointed out the hours, but also, by dropping small balls on a bell, struck them; and, at the same instant, threw open as many little doors, to let out an equal number of horsemen. *Ann. Reg. Franc. Pip. Caroli, Sfc. ad ann.* 807. *Weidler*, p. 205.

12. *their beards to be burnt.* The loss of the beard, from the earliest ages, was accounted highly disgraceful. An instance occurs, in the Tales of Inatulla, of one being *singed off,* as a mulct on the owner, for having failed to explain a question propounded; and, in the Arabian Nights, a proclamation may be seen similar to this of Vathek. Vol. I. p. 268. Vol. II. p. 228.

13. *Giaour.* Means *infidel.*

14. *the Divan.* This was both the supreme council and court of justice, at which the caliphs of the race of the Abassides assisted in person, to redress the injuries of every appellant. *D'Herbelot,* p. 298.

15. *the prime vizir.* Vazir, vezir, or as we express it, vizir, literally signifies a *porter;* and, by metaphor, the minister who bears the principal burthen of the state, generally called the sublime Porte.

16. *The Meuzins and their minarets.* Valid, the son of Abdalmalek, was the first who erected a *minaret,* or turret; and this he placed on the grand mosque at Damascus; for the *meuzin,* or crier, to announce from it, the hour of prayer. This practice has constantly been kept to this day. *D'Herbelot,* p. 576.

17. *Soliman Ben Daoud.* The name of David in Hebrew is composed of the letter ו *Vau* between two ד *Daleths* דוד; and according to the Massoretic points ought to be pronounced *David.* Having no v consonant in their tongue, the Septuagint substituted the letter b for v, and wrote Δαβιδ, *Dabid.* The Syriac reads *Dad* or *Dod;* and the Arabs articulate *Daoud.*

18. *with the grin of an ogre.* Thus, in the history of the punished vizir:—"The prince heard enough to convince him of his danger, and then perceived that the lady, who called herself the daughter of an *Indian* king, was an ogress, wife to one of those *savage demons,* called ogre, who stay in remote places, and make use of a thousand wiles to surprize and devour passengers." *Arab. Nights,* vol. I. p. 56.

19. *mutes.* It has been usual, in eastern courts, from time immemorial, to retain a number of mutes. These are not only employed to amuse the monarch, but also to instruct his pages, in an art to us little known, that of communicating their thoughts by signs, lest the sounds of their voices

should disturb the sovereign. *Habesci's State of the Ottoman Empire,* p. 164. The mutes are also the secret instruments of his private vengeance, in carrying the fatal string.

20. *Prayer announced at break of day.* The stated seasons of public prayer, in the twenty-four hours, were five: day-break, noon, mid-time between noon and sun-set, immediately as the sun leaves the horizon, and an hour and half after it is down.

21. *mummies. Moumia* (from *moum,* wax and tallow) signifies the flesh of the human body preserved in the sand, after having been embalmed and wrapt in cerements. They are frequently found in the sepulchres of Egypt; but most of the Oriental mummies are brought from a cavern near Abin, in Persia. *D'Herbelot,* p. 647.

22. *a parchment.* Parchments of the like mysterious import are frequently mentioned in the works of the Eastern writers. One in particular, amongst the Arabians, is held in high veneration. It was written by Ali, and Giafar Sadek, in mystic characters, and is said to contain the destiny of the Mahometan religion, and the great events which are to happen previous to the end of the world. This parchment is of *camel's skin.*

23. *Istakhar.* This city was the ancient Persepolis and capital of Persia, under the kings of the three first races. The author of Lebtarikh writes that Kischtab there established his abode, erected several temples to the element of fire, and hewed out, for himself and his successors, sepulchres in the rocks of the mountain contiguous to the city. The ruins of columns and broken figures which still remain, defaced as they were by Alexander, and mutilated by time, plainly evince that those ancient potentates had chosen it for the place of their interment.

24. *the talismans of Soliman.* The most famous *talisman* of the East, and which could control even the arms and magic of the dives, or giants, was *Mohur Solimani,* the seal or ring of Soliman Jared, fifth monarch of the world after Adam. By means of it, the possessor had the entire command, not only of the elements, but also of demons, and every created being. *Richardson's Dissertation.* p. 272. *D'Herbelot,* p. 820.

25. *pre-adamite sultans.* These monarchs, which were seventy-two in number, are said to have governed each a distinct species of rational beings, prior to the existence of Adam.

26. *beware how thou enterest any dwelling.* Strange as this injunction may seem, it is by no means incongruous to the customs of the country. Dr. Pocock mentions his travelling with the train of the Governor of Faiume, who, instead of lodging in a village that was near, preferred to pass the night in a grove of palm-trees. *Travels*, vol. I. p. 56.

27. *every bumper he ironically quaffed to the health of Mahomet.* There are innumerable proofs that the Grecian custom, συμπιειν κυαθιζομενους, prevailed amongst the Arabs; but had these been wanted, Carathis could not be supposed a stranger to it. The practice was to hail the gods, in the first place; and then, those who were held in the highest veneration.

28. *the ass of Balaam, the dog of the seven sleepers, and the other animals admitted into the paradise of Mahomet.* It was a tenet of the Mussulman creed, that all animals would be raised again, and many of them honoured with admission to paradise. The story of the seven sleepers, borrowed from Christian legends, was this:—In the days of the Emperor Decius, there were certain Ephesian youths of a good family, who, to avoid the flames of persecution, fled to a secret cavern, and there slept for a number of years. In their flight towards the cave, they were followed by a dog, which, when they attempted to drive him back, said: *"I love those who are dear unto God; go sleep, therefore, and I will guard you."*—For this dog the Mahometans retain so profound a reverence, that their harshest sarcasm against a covetous person, is, "He would not throw a bone to the dog of the seven sleepers." It is even said, that their superstition induces them to write his name upon the letters they send to a distance, as a kind of talisman to secure them a safe conveyance. *Religious Ceremonies*, vol. VII. p. 74, n. *Sale's Koran*, ch. xviii. *and notes.*

29. *painting the eyes of the Circassians.* It was an ancient custom in the East, which still continues, to tinge the eyes of women, particularly those of a fair complexion, with an impalpable powder, prepared chiefly from crude

antimony, and called *surmeh*. Ebni'l Motezz, in a passage translated by Sir W. Jones, hath not only ascertained its *purple* colour, but also likened the *violet* to it.

> Viola collegit folia sua, similia
>
> Collyrionigro, quod bibit lachrymas die discessus,
>
> Velut si esset super vasa in quibus fulgent
>
> Primæ ignis flammulæ in sulphuris extremis partibus.

This pigment, when applied to the inner surface of the lids, communicates to the eye (especially if seen by the light of lamps) so tender and fascinating a languor, as no language is competent to express. Hence the epithet Ιοβλεφαρος, violet-colour eye-lids, attributed by the Greeks to the goddess of beauty.

30. *Rocnabad.* The stream thus denominated, flows near the city of Schiraz. Its waters are uncommonly pure and limpid, and its banks swarded with the finest verdure. Its praises are celebrated by Hafez, in an animated song, which Sir W. Jones has admirably translated:—

> Boy, let yon liquid ruby flow,
>
> And bid thy pensive heart be glad,
>
> Whate'er the frowning zealots say:
>
> Tell them, their Eden cannot shew
>
> A stream so clear as Rocnabad,
>
> A bower so sweet as Mosella.

Mosella was an oratory on the banks of Rocnabad.

31. *Moullahs.* Those amongst the Mahometans who were bred to the law, had this title; and the judges of cities and provinces were taken from their order.

32. *the sacred Cahaba.* That part of the temple at Mecca which is chiefly revered, and, indeed, gives a sanctity to the rest, is a square stone building, the length of which, from north to south, is twenty-four cubits; and its breadth, from east to west, twenty-three. The door is on the east side, and stands about four cubits from the ground, the floor being level with the threshold. The Cahaba has a double roof, supported internally by three

octangular pillars of aloes-wood; between which, on a bar of iron, hangs a row of silver lamps. The outside is covered with rich black damask, adorned with an embroidered band of gold. This hanging, which is changed every year, was formerly sent by the caliphs. *Sale's Preliminary Discourse*, p. 152.

33. *regale these pious poor souls with my good wine from Schiraz.* The prohibition of wine in the Koran is so rigidly observed by the conscientious, especially if they have performed the pilgrimage to Mecca, that they deem it sinful to press grapes for the purpose of making it, and even to use the money arising from its sale. *Chardin, Voy. de Perse, tom.* II. p. 212.—*Schiraz* was famous in the East, for its wines of different sorts, but particularly for its *red*, which was esteemed more highly than even the white wine of *Kismische.*

34. *the most stately tulips of the East.* The tulip is a flower of eastern growth, and there held in great estimation. Thus, in an ode of Mesihi:—"The edge of the bower is filled with the light of Ahmed: among the plants, the fortunate *tulips* represent his companions."

35. *certain cages of ladies.* There are many passages of the Moallakat in which these *cages* are fully described. Thus, in the poem of Lebeid:—"How were thy tender affections raised, when the damsels of the tribe departed; when they hid themselves in carriages of cotton, like antelopes in their lair, and the tents as they were struck gave piercing sound!

"They were concealed in vehicles, whose sides were well covered with awnings and carpets, with fine-spun curtains and pictured veils."

Again, Zohair:—

"They are mounted in carriages covered with costly awnings, and with rose-coloured veils, the lining of which have the hue of crimson andem-wood." *Moallakat, by Sir W. Jones*, p. 46. 35. *See also Lady M. W. Montague*, Let. xxvi.

36. *the locusts were heard from the thickets on the plain of Catoul.* These insects are of the same species with the τιττιξ of the Greeks, and the *cicada* of the Latins. The locusts are mentioned in Pliny, b. 11. 29. They were so called

from *loco usto*, because the havoc they made wherever they passed left behind the appearance of a place desolated by fire. How could then the commentators of Vathek say that they are called *locusts*, from their having been so denominated by the first English settlers in America?

37. *Vathek—with two little pages.* "All the pages of the seraglio are sons of Christians made slaves in time of war, in their most tender age. The incursions of robbers in the confines of Circassia, afford the means of supplying the seraglio, even in times of peace." *Habesci's State of the Ottoman Empire,* p. 157. That the pages here mentioned were *Circassians,* appears from the description of their complexion:—*more fair than the enamel of Franguistan.*

38. *Confectioners and cooks.* What their precise number might have been in Vathek's establishment, it is not now easy to determine; but, in the household of the present Grand Seignor, there are not fewer than a hundred and ninety. *Habesci's State,* p. 145.

39. *torches were lighted.* Mr. Marsden relates, in his *History of Sumatra,* that tigers prove most fatal and destructive enemies to the inhabitants, particularly in their journies; and adds, that the numbers annually slain by those rapacious tyrants of the woods, is almost incredible. As these tremendous enemies are alarmed at the appearance of fire, it is usual for the natives to carry a splendid kind of torch, chiefly to frighten them; and, also, to make a blaze with wood, in different parts, round their villages, p. 149.

40. *One of the forests of cedar, that bordered their way, took fire.* Accidents of this kind, in Persia, are not unfrequent. "It was an ancient practice with the kings and great men to set fire to large bunches of dry combustibles, fastened round wild beasts and birds, which being then let loose, naturally fled to the woods for shelter, and caused destructive conflagrations." *Richardson's Dissertat,* p. 185.

41. *hath seen some part of our bodies; and, what is worse, our very faces.* "I was informed," writes Dr. Cooke, "that the Persian women, in general, would sooner expose to public view any part of their bodies than their faces." *Voyages and Travels,* vol. II. p. 443.

42. *cakes baked in silver ovens for his royal mouth.* Portable ovens were a part of the furniture of eastern travellers. St. Jerom (on Lament, v. 10) hath particularly described them. The Caliph's were of the same kind, only substituting silver for brass. Dr. Pocock mentions his having been entertained in an Arabian camp with cakes baked for him. In what the peculiarity of the royal bread consisted, it is not easy to determine; but, in one of the Arabian Tales, a woman, to gratify her utmost desire, wishes to become the wife of the sultan's baker; assigning for the reason, that she might have her fill of that bread, which is called the sultan's. Vol. IV. p. 269.

43. *vases of snow; and grapes from the banks of the Tigris.* It was customary in eastern climates, and especially in the sultry season, to carry, when journeying, supplies of snow. These *æstivæ nives* (as Mamertinus styles them) being put into separate vases, were, by that means, better kept from the air, as no more was opened at once than might suffice for immediate use. To preserve the whole from solution, the vessels that contained it were secured in packages of straw. Gesta Dei, p. 1098.—Vathek's ancestor, the Caliph Mahadi, in the pilgrimage to Mecca, which he undertook from ostentation rather than devotion, loaded upon camels so prodigious a quantity as was not only sufficient for himself and his attendants, amidst the burning sands of Arabia; but, also, to preserve, in their natural freshness, the various fruits he took with him, and to ice all their drink whilst he staid at Mecca: the greater part of whose inhabitants had never seen snow till then. *Anecdotes Arabes,* p. 326.

44. *horrible Kaf.* This mountain, which, in reality, is no other than Caucasus, was supposed to surround the earth, like a ring encompassing a finger. The sun was believed to rise from one of its eminences, (as over Oeta, by the Latin poets) and to set on the opposite; whence, *from Kaf to Kaf,* signified from one extremity of the earth to the other. The fabulous historians of the East affirm, that this mountain was founded upon a stone, called *sakhrat,* one grain of which, according to Lokman, would enable the possessor to work wonders. This stone is further described as the pivot of the earth; and said to be one vast emerald, from the refraction of whose beams, the

heavens derive their azure. It is added, that whenever God would excite an earthquake, he commands the stone to move one of its fibres, (which supply in it the office of nerves) and, that being moved, the part of the earth connected with it, quakes, is convulsed, and sometimes expands. Such is the philosophy of the Koran!—The Tarikh Tabari, written in Persian, analagous to the same tradition, relates, that, were it not for this emerald, the earth would be liable to perpetual commotions and unfit for the abode of mankind. To arrive at the Kaf, a vast region, far from the sun and summer-gale, must be traversed. Over this dark and cheerless desart, the way is inextricable, without the direction of supernatural guidance. Here the dives or giants were confined after their defeat by the first heroes of the human race; and here, also, the peries, or faeries, are supposed in ordinary to reside. Sukrage, the giant, was King of Kaf, and had Rucail, one of the children of Adam, for his prime minister. The giant Argenk, likewise, from the time that Tahamurah made war upon him, reigned here, and reared a superb palace in the city of Aherman, with galleries, on whose walls were painted the creatures that inhabited the world prior to the formation of Adam. *D'Herbelot*, p. 230, &c. &c.

45. *the simurgh.* That wonderful bird of the East, concerning which so many marvels are told, was not only endowed with reason, but possessed also the knowledge of every language. Hence it may be concluded to have been a dive in a borrowed form. This creature relates of itself that it had seen the great revolution of seven thousand years, twelve times commence and close; and that, in its duration, the world had been seven times void of inhabitants, and as often replenished. The simurgh is represented as a great friend to the race of Adam, and not less inimical to the dives. Tahamurath and Aherman were apprised by its predictions of all that was destined to befal them, and from it they obtained the promise of assistance in every undertaking. Armed with the buckler of Gian Ben Gian, Tahamurath was borne by it through the air, over the dark desert, to Kaf. From its bosom his helmet was crested with plumes, which the most renowned warriors have ever since worn. In every conflict the simurgh was invulnerable,

and the heroes it favoured never failed of success. Though possessed of power sufficient to exterminate its foes, yet the exertion of that power was supposed to be forbidden.—Sadi, a serious author, gives it as an instance of the universality of Providence, that the simurgh, notwithstanding its immense bulk, is at no loss for sustenance on the mountain of Kaf.

46. *afrits.* These were a kind of Medusae, or Lamiæ, supposed to be the most terrible and cruel of all the orders of the dives. *D'Herbelot,* p. 60.

47. *Tablets fraught with preternatural qualities.* Mr. Richardson observes, "that in the East, men of rank in general carried with them pocket astronomical tables, which they consulted on every affair of moment." These tablets, however, were of the *magical* kind; and such as often occur in works of romance. Thus, in Boiardo, Orlando receives, from the father of the youth he had rescued, "a book that would solve all doubts:" and, in Ariosto, Logistilla bestows upon Astolpho a similar directory.

48. *dwarfs.* Such unfortunate beings, as are thus "curtailed of fair proportion," have been, for ages, an appendage of Eastern grandeur. One part of their office consists in the instruction of the pages, but their principal duty is the amusement of their master. If a dwarf happen to be a mute, he is much esteemed; but if he be also an eunuch, he is regarded as a prodigy; and no pains or expense are spared to obtain him. *Habesci's State of the Ottoman Empire,* p. 164, &c.

49. *A small spring supplies us with water for the abdest, and we daily repeat prayers, &c.* Amongst the indispensable rules of the Mahometan faith, ablution is one of the chief. This rite is divided into three kinds. The first, performed before prayers, is called *abdest.* It begins with washing both hands, and repeating these words:—"Praised be Alla, who created clean water, and gave it the virtue to purify: he also hath rendered our faith conspicuous." This done, water is taken in the right hand thrice, and the mouth being washed, the worshipper subjoins: "I pray thee, O Lord, to let me taste of that water, which thou hast given to thy Prophet Mahomet in paradise, more fragrant than musk, whiter than milk, sweeter than honey: and which has the power to quench for ever, the thirst of him that drinks it."

This petition is accompanied with sniffing a little water into the nose; the face is then three times washed, and behind the ears; after which, water is taken with both hands, beginning with the right, and thrown to the elbow. The washing of the crown next follows, and the apertures of the ear with the thumbs: afterward the neck with all the fingers; and, finally, the feet. In this last operation, it is held sufficient to wet the sandal only. At each ceremonial a suitable petition is offered, and the whole concludes with this: "Hold me up firmly, O Lord! and suffer not my foot to slip, that I may not fall from the bridge into hell." Nothing can be more exemplary than the attention with which these rites are performed. If an involuntary cough or sneeze interrupt them, the whole service is begun anew, and that as often as it happens. *Habesci*, p. 91, &c.

50. *the bells of a cafila.* A cafila, or caravan, according to Pitts, is divided into distinct companies, at the head of which an officer, or person of distinction, is carried in a kind of horse litter, and followed by a sumpter camel, loaded with his treasure. This camel hath a bell fastened to either side, the sound of which may be heard at a considerable distance. Others have bells on their necks and their legs, to solace them when drooping with heat and fatigue.—Inatulla also, in his tales, hath a similar reference:—"the bells of the cafila may be rung in the thirsty desert." vol. II. p. 15. These small bells were known at Rome from the earliest times, and called from their sounds *tintinnabulum*. Phædrus gives us a lively description of the mule carrying the fiscal monies; *clarumque collo jactans tintinnabulum*. Book II. fabl. vii.

51. *Deggial.* This word signifies properly a liar and impostor, but is applied, by Mahometan writers, to their *Antichrist*. He is described as having but one eye and eye-brow, and on his forehead the radicals of *cafer* or *infidel* are said to be impressed. According to the traditions of the faithful, his first appearance will be between Irak and Syria, mounted on an ass. Seventy thousand Jews from Ispahan are expected to follow him. His continuance on earth is to be forty days. All places are to be destroyed by him and his emissaries, except *Mecca* or *Medina;* which will be protected by angels from the general overthrow. At last, however, he will be slain by Jesus,

who is to encounter him at the gate of Lud. *D'Herbelot*, p. 282. *Sale's Prelim. Disc.* p. 106.

52. *sugar.* Dr. Pocock mentions the sugar-cane as a great desert in Egypt; and adds, that, besides coarse loaf sugar and sugar candy, it yields a third sort, remarkably fine, which is sent to the Grand Seignor, and prepared only for himself. *Travels*, vol. I. p. 183. 204. The jeweller's son, in the story of the third Calender, desires the prince to fetch some *melon* and *sugar*, that he might refresh himself with them. *Arab. Nights*, vol. I. p. 159.

53. *red characters.* The laws of Draco are recorded by Plutarch, in his life of Solon, to have been written in blood. If more were meant by this expression, than that those laws were of a sanguinary nature, they will furnish the earliest instance of the use of red characters; which were afterwards considered as appropriate to supreme authority, and employed to denounce some requisition or threatening designed to strike terror.

54. *thy body shall be spit upon.* There was no mark of contempt amongst the Easterns so ignominious as this. *Arab. Nights* vol. I. p. 115. Vol. IV. p. 275.

55. *bats will nestle in thy belly.* Bats, in those countries, were very abundant; and, both from their numbers and size, held in abhorrence. See what is related of them by Thevenot, Part I. p. 132, 3. *Egmont and Hayman*, vol. II. p. 87, and other travellers in the East.

56. *the Bismillah.* This word (which is prefixed to every chapter of the Koran, except the ninth) signifies, "in the name of the most merciful God."—It became not the initiatory formula of prayer, till the time of Moez the Fatimitc. *D'Herbelot*, p. 326.

57. *a magnificent tecthtrevan.* This kind of moving throne, though more common, at present, than in the days of Vathek, is still confined to persons of the highest rank.

58. *baths of rose water.* The use of perfumed waters for the purpose of bathing is of an early origin in the East, where every odoriferous plant breathes a richer fragrance than is known to our more humid climates. The rose which yields this lotion is, according to Hasselquist, of a beautiful pale bluish colour, double, large as a man's fist, and more exquisite in scent

than any other species. The quantities of this water distilled annually at Fajhum, and carried to distant countries, is immense. The mode of conveying it is in vessels of copper, coated with wax. *Voyag.* p. 248.

59. *lamb à la crême.* No dish amongst the Easterns was more generally admired. The Caliph Abdolmelek, at a splendid entertainment, to which whoever came was welcome, asked Amrou, the son of Hareth, what kind of meat he preferred to all others. The old man answered: "An ass's neck, well seasoned and roasted."—"But what say you," replied the Caliph, "to the leg or shoulder of a lamb *à la crême?*" and added, "How sweetly we live if a shadow would last!" *M.S. Laud. Numb.* 161. A. *Ockley's Hist. of the Saracens,* vol. II. p. 277.

60. *made the dwarfs dance against their will.* Ali Chelebi al Moufti, in a treatise on the subject, held that dancing, after the example of the derviches, who made it a part of their devotion, was allowable. But in this opinion he was deemed to be heterodox; for Mahometans, in general, place dancing amongst the things that are forbidden. *D'Herbelot,* p. 98.

61. *durst not refuse the commander of the faithful.* The mandates of Oriental potentates have ever been accounted irresistible. Hence the submission of these devotees to the will of the Caliph. *Esther* i. 19. *Daniel* vi. 8. *Ludeke Expos, brevis,* p. 60.

62. *properly lubricated with the balm of Mecca.* Unguents, for reasons sufficiently obvious, have been of general use in hot climates. According to Pliny, "at the time of the Trojan war, they consisted of oils perfumed with the odours of flowers, and, chiefly, of roses."—Hasselquist speaks of oil, impregnated with the tuberose and jessamine; but the unguent here mentioned was preferred to every other. Lady M. W. Montagu, desirous to try its effects, seems to have suffered materially from having improperly applied it.

63. *black eunuchs, sabre in hand.* In this manner the apartments of the ladies were constantly guarded. Thus, in the story of the enchanted horse, Firouz Schah, traversing a strange palace by night, entered a room, "and, by the light of a lanthorn, saw that the persons he had heard snoring, were black eunuchs with naked sabres by them; which was enough to inform him

that this was the guard-chamber of some queen or princess." *Arabian Nights*, vol. IV. p. 189.

64. *to let down the great swing*. The swing was an exercise much used in the apartments of the Eastern ladies, and not only contributed to their amusement, but also to their health. *Tales of Inatulla*, vol. I. p. 259.

65. *melodious Philomel, I am thy rose*. The passion of the nightingale for the rose is celebrated over all the East. Thus, Meshii, as translated by Sir W. Jones:

Come, charming maid, and hear thy poet sing,

Thyself the rose, and he the bird of Spring:

Love bids him sing, and Love will be obey'd,

Be gay: too soon the flowers of Spring will fade.

66. *oil spilt in breaking the lamps*. It appears from Thevenot, that illuminations were usual on the arrival of a stranger, and he mentions, on an occasion of this sort, two hundred lamps being lighted. The quantity of oil, therefore, spilt on the margin of the bath, may be easily accounted for, from this custom.

67. *calenders*. These were a sort of men amongst the Mahometans, who abandoned father and mother, wife and children, relations and possessions, to wander through the world, under a pretence of religion, entirely subsisting on the fortuitous bounty of those they had the address to dupe. *D'Herbelot, Suppl.* p. 204.

68. *santons*. A body of religionists who were also called *abdals*, and pretended to be inspired with the most enthusiastic raptures of divine love. They were regarded by the vulgar as *saints*. *Olearius*, tom. I. p. 97 1. *D'Herbelot*, p. 5.

69. *derviches*. The term *dervich* signifies a *poor man*, and is the general appellation by which a Mahometan monk is named. There are, however, discriminations that distinguish this class from the others already mentioned. They are bound by no vow of poverty, they abstained not from marriage, and, whenever disposed, they may relinquish both their blue shirt and profession. *D'Herbelot, Suppl.* 214.—It is observable that these different orders, though not established till the reign of Nasser al Samani, are notwithstanding mentioned by our author as coeval with

Vathek, and by the author of the Arabian Nights, as existing in the days of Haroun al Raschid: so that the Arabian fabulists appear as inattentive to chronological exactness in points of this sort, as our immortal dramatist himself.

70. *Bramins.* These constitute the principal caste of the Indians, according to whose doctrine *Brahma*, from whom they are called, is the first of the three created beings, by whom the world was made. This Brahma is said to have communicated to the Indians four books, in which all the sciences and ceremonies of their religion are comprized. The word Brahma, in the Indian language, signifies *pervading all things*. The Brahmins lead a life of most rigid abstinence, refraining not only from the use, but even the touch, of animal food; and are equally exemplary for their contempt of pleasures and devotion to philosophy and religion. *D'Herbelot*, p. 212. *Bruckeri Hist. Philosoph.* tom. I. p. 194.

71. *faquirs.* This sect are a kind of religious anchorets, who spend their whole lives in the severest austerities and mortification. It is almost impossible for the imagination to form an extravagance that has not been practised by some of them, to torment themselves. As their reputation for sanctity rises in proportion to their sufferings, those amongst them are reverenced the most, who are most ingenious in the invention of tortures, and persevering in enduring them. Hence some have persisted in sitting or standing for years together in one unvaried posture; supporting an almost intolerable burden; dragging the most cumbrous chains; exposing their naked bodies to the scorching sun, and hanging with the head downward before the fiercest fires. *Relig. Ceremon.* vol. III. p. 264, &c. *White's Sermons*, p. 504.

72. *some that cherished vermin.* In this attachment they were not singular. The Emperor Julian not only discovered the same partiality, but celebrated, with visible complacency, the shaggy and *populous* beard, which he fondly cherished; and even "The Historian of the Roman Empire," affirms "that the little animal is a beast familiar to man, and signifies love." Vol. II. p. 343.

73. *Visnow and Ixhora.* Two deities of the Hindoos. The traditions of their

votaries are, probably, allegorical; but without a key to disclose their mystic import, they are little better than senseless jargon; and, with the key, downright nonsense.

74. *talapoins.* This order, which abounds in Siam, Laos, Pegu, and other countries, consists of different classes, and both sexes, but chiefly of men. *Relig. Ceremon.* vol. IV. p. 62, &c.

75. *objects of pity were sure to swarm around him.* Ludeke mentions the practice of bringing those who were suffering under any calamity, or had lost the use of their limbs, &c. into public, for the purpose of exciting compassion. On an occasion, therefore, of this sort, when Fakreddin, like a pious Mussulman, was publicly to distribute his alms, and the commander of the faithful to make his appearance, such an assemblage might well be expected. The Eastern custom of regaling a convention of this kind is of great antiquity, as is evident from the parable of the king, in the Gospels, who entertained the maimed, the lame, and the blind; nor was it discontinued when Dr. Pocock visited the East. Vol. I. p. 182.

76. *small plates of abominations.* The Koran hath established several distinctions relative to different kinds of food, in imitation of the Jewish prescriptions; and many Mahometans are so scrupulous as not to touch the flesh of any animal over which, *in articulo mortis*, the butcher had omitted to pronounce the *Bismillah. Relig. Cerem.* vol. VII. p. 110.

77. *Sinai.* This mountain is deemed by Mahometans the noblest of all others, and even regarded with the highest veneration, because the divine law was promulgated from it. *D'Herbelot*, p. 812.

78. *Peries.* The word *Peri*, in the Persian language, signifies that beautiful race of creatures which constitutes the link between angels and men.—*See endnote 9.*

79. *butterflies of Cachemire.* The same insects are celebrated in an unpublished poem of Mesihi. Sir Anthony Shirley relates, that it was customary in Persia "to hawke after butterflies with sparrows, made to that use, and stares."—It is, perhaps, to this amusement that our Author alludes in the context.

80. *Megnoun and Leilah.* These personages are esteemed amongst the Arabians as the most beautiful, chaste, and impassioned of lovers; and their amours have been celebrated with all the charms of verse in every Oriental language. The Mahometans regard them, and the poetical records of their love, in the same light as the Bridegroom and Spouse, and the Song of Songs are regarded by the Jews. *D'Herbelot*, p. 573.

81. *dart the lance in the chace.* Throwing the lance was a favourite pastime with the young Arabians; and so expert were they in this practice (which prepared them for the mightier conflicts, both of the chace and war) that they could bear oft' a ring on the points of their javelins. *Richardson's Dissertat.* p. 198. 281.

82. *The two brothers had mutually engaged their children to each other.* Contracts of this nature were frequent amongst the Arabians. Another instance occurs in the Story of Noureddin Ali and Benreddin Hassan.

83. *Nouronihar loved her cousin, more than her own beautiful eyes.* This mode of expression not only occurs in the sacred writers, but also in the Greek and Roman. Thus Catullus says: Quem plus illa oculis suis amabat.

84. *the same long languishing looks.* So Ariosto:

————negri occhi,————

Pietosi a riguardare, a mover parchi.

85. *Shaddukian and Ambreabad.* These were two cities of the Peries, in the imaginary region of *Ginnistan*, the former signifies *pleasure* and *desire*, the latter *the city of Ambergris. See Richardson's Dissertat.* p. 169.

86. *a spoon of cocknos.* The cocknos is a bird whose beak is much esteemed for its beautiful polish, and sometimes used as a spoon. Thus, in the History of Atalmulck and Zelica Begum, it was employed for a similar purpose:— "Zelica having called for refreshment, six old slaves instantly brought in and distributed *Mahramas*, and then served about in a great bason of Martabam, a salad *made of herbs of various kinds, citron juice, and the pith of cucumbers.* They served it first to the Princess in *a cocknos' beak:* she took a beak of the salad, eat it, and gave another to the next slave that sat by her on her right hand; which slave did as her mistress had done."

87. *Goules.* Goul, or *ghul,* in Arabic, signifies any terrifying object, which deprives people of the use of their senses. Hence it became the appellative of that species of monster which was supposed to haunt forests, cemeteries, and other lonely places; and believed not only to tear in pieces the living, but to dig up and devour the dead. *Richardson's Dissert.* p. 174. 274.

88. *feathers of the heron, all sparkling carbuncles.* Panaches of this kind are amongst the attributes of Eastern royalty. *Tales of Inatulla,* vol. ii. p. 205.

89. *the carbuncle of Giamschid.* This mighty potentate was the fourth sovereign of the dynasty of the Pischadians, and brother or nephew to Tahamurath. His proper name was *giam* or *gem,* and *sched,* which in the language of the ancient Persians denominated the sun: an addition, ascribed by some to the majesty of his person, and by others to the splendour of his actions. One of the most magnificent monuments of his reign was the city of Istakhar, of which Tahamurath had laid the foundations. This city, at present called *Gihil-,* or *Tchil-minar,* from the forty columns reared in it by Homai, or (according to our author and others) by Soliman Ben Daoud, was known to the Greeks by the name of Persepolis: and there is still extant in the East a tradition, that, when Alexander burnt the edifices of the Persian kings, seven stupendous structures of Giamschid were consumed with his palace.

90. *the torches were extinguished.* To the union here prefigured, the following lines may be applied:

Non *Hymenaeus* adest illi, non gratia lecto;

Eumenides tenuere faces de funere raptas:

Eumenides stravere torum.

91. *She clapped her hands.* This was the ordinary method in the East of calling the attendants in waiting. See *Arabian Nights,* vol. I. p. 5. 106. 193, &c.

92. *Funeral vestments were prepared; their bodies washed, &c.* The rites here practised had obtained from the earliest ages. Most of them may be found in Homer and the other poets of Greece. Lucian describes the dead in his time as washed, perfumed, vested, and crowned, with the flowers most in season; or, according to other writers, those in particular which the deceased were wont to prefer.

93. *all instruments of music were broken.* Thus, in the Arabian Nights: "Haroun al Raschid wept over Schemselnihar, and, before he left the room, ordered all the musical instruments to be broken." Vol. II. p. 196.

94. *Imans began to recite their prayers.* An iman is the principal priest of a mosque. It was the office of the imans to precede the bier, praying as the procession moved on. *Relig. Cerem.* vol. VII. p. 117.

95. *the angel of death had opened the portal of some other world.* The name of this exterminating angel is Azrael, and his office is to conduct the dead to the abode assigned them; which is said by some to be near the place of their interment. Such was the office of Mercury in the Grecian Mythology. *Sale's Prelim. Disc.* p. 101. *Hyde in notis ad Bobov.* p. 19. *R. Elias, in Tishbi. Buxtorf Synag. Jud. et Lexic. Talmud. Homer. Odyss.*

96. *Monker and Nekir.* These are two black angels of a tremendous appearance, who examine the departed on the subject of his faith: by whom, if he give not a satisfactory account, he is sure to be cudgelled with maces of red-hot iron, and tormented more variously than words can describe. *Relig. Ceremon.* vol. VII. p. 59. 68. 118. vol. V. p. 290. *Sale's Prelim. Disc.* p. 101.

97. *the fatal bridge.* This bridge, called in Arabick *al Siral,* and said to extend over the infernal gulph, is represented as narrower than a spider's web, and sharper than the edge of a sword. Yet the paradise of Mahomet can be entered by no other avenue. Those indeed who have behaved well need not be alarmed; mixed characters will find it difficult; but the wicked soon miss their standing, and plunge headlong into the abyss. *Pocock in Port. Mos.* p. 282, &c.

98. *a certain series of years.* According to the tradition from the Prophet, not less than nine hundred, nor more than seven thousand.

99. *the sacred camel.* It was an article of the Mahometan creed, that all animals would be raised again, and some of them admitted into paradise. The animal here mentioned appears to have been one of those *white-winged* camels *caparisoned with gold,* which Ali affirmed would be provided to convey the faithful. *Relig. Cer.* vol. VII. p. 70. *Sale's Prelim. Disc.* p. 112. *Al Janheri. Ebno'l Athir,* &c.

100. *the Caliph presented himself to the emir in a new light.* The propensity of a vicious person, in affliction, to seek consolation from the ceremonies of religion, is an exquisite trait in the character of Vathek.

101. *wine hoarded up in bottles, prior to the birth of Mahomet.* The prohibition of wine by the Prophet materially diminished its consumption, within the limits of his own dominions. Hence a reserve of it might be expected, of the age here specified. The custom of hoarding wine was not unknown to the Persians, though not so often practised by them, as by the Greeks and the Romans.

"I purchase" (says Lebeid) "the old liquor, at a dear rate, in dark leathern bottles, long reposited; or in casks black with pitch, whose seals I break, and then fill the cheerful goblet." *Moallakat*, p. 53.

102. *excavated ovens in the rock.* As substitutes for the portable ovens, which were lost.

103. *the confines of some cemetery.* Places of interment in the East were commonly situated in scenes of solitude. We read of one in the history of the first calender, abounding with so many monuments, that four days were successively spent in it without the inquirer being able to find the tomb he looked for: and, from the story of Ganem, it appears that the doors of these cemeteries were often left open. *Arabian Nights*, vol. II. p. 112.

104. *a Myrabolan comfit.* The invention of this confection is attributed by M. Cardonne to Avicenna, but there is abundant reason, exclusive of our author's authority, to suppose it of a much earlier origin. Both the Latins and Greeks were acquainted with the balsam, and the tree that produced it was indigenous in various parts of Arabia.

105. *blue fishes.* Fishes of the same colour are mentioned in the Arabian Nights; and, like these, were endowed with the gift of speech.

106. *astrolabes.* The mention of the astrolabe may be deemed incompatible, at first view, with chronological exactness, as there is no instance of any being constructed by a Mussulman, till after the time of Vathek. It may, however, be remarked, to go no higher, that Sinesius, bishop of Ptolemais, invented one in the fifth century; and that Carathis was not only herself a Greek, but also cultivated those sciences which the good Mussulmans of

her time all held in abhorrence. *Bailly, Hist. de l'Astronom. Moderne*, tom. I. p. 563. 573.

107. *On the banks of the stream, hives and oratories.* The bee is an insect held in high veneration amongst the Mahometans, it being pointed out in the Koran, "for a sign unto the people that understand." It has been said, in the same sense: "Go to the ant, thou sluggard," *Prov.* vi. 6. The santons, therefore, who inhabit the fertile banks of Rocnabad, are not less famous for their hives than their oratories. *D'Herbelot*, p. 717.

108. *Shieks, cadis.* Shieks are the chiefs of the societies of derviches: cadis are the magistrates of a town or city.

109. *Asses in bridles of riband inscribed from the Koran.* As the judges of Israel in ancient days rode on white asses, so amongst the Mahometans, those that affect an extraordinary sanctity, use the same animal in preference to the horse. Sir John Chardin observed in various parts of the East, that their reins, as here represented, were of silk, with the name of God, or other inscriptions upon them. *Ludeke Expos. brevis*, p. 49. *Chardin's MS.* cited by Harmer.

110. *Eblis.* D'Herbelot supposes this title to have been a corruption of the Greek Διαβολος *diabolos*. It was the appellation conferred by the Arabians upon the prince of the apostate angels, and appears more likely to originate from the Hebrew רבה *hebel*, vanity, pride.—*See endnote 114*, "creatures of clay."

111. *compensate for thy impieties by an exemplary life.* It is an established article of the Mussulman creed, that the actions of mankind are all weighed in a vast unerring balance, and the future condition of the agents determined according to the preponderance of evil or good. This fiction, which seems to have been borrowed from the Jews, had probably its origin in the figurative language of scripture. Thus, Psalm lxii. 9. Surely men of low degree are vanity, and men of high degree are a lie: to be laid in the balance, they are altogether lighter than vanity:—and, in Daniel, the sentence against the King of Babylon, inscribed on the wall: Thou art weighed in the balance, and found wanting.

112. *Balkis.* This was the Arabian name of the Queen of Sheba, who went from the south to hear the wisdom and admire the glory of Solomon. The Koran represents her as a worshipper of fire. Solomon is said not only to have entertained her with the greatest magnificence, but also to have raised her to his bed and his throne. *Al Koran*, ch. XXVII. and *Sale's notes*. *D'Herbelot*, p. 182.

113. *Ouranbad.* This monster is represented as a fierce flying hydra, and belongs to the same class with the *rakshe* whose ordinary food was serpents and dragons; the *soham*, which had the head of a horse, with four eyes, and the body of a flame-coloured dragon; the *syl*, a basilisk with a face resembling the human, but so tremendous that no mortal could bear to behold it; the *ejder*, and others. See these respective titles in *Richardson's Persian, Arabic, and English Dictionary.*

114. *Creatures of clay.* Nothing could have been more appositely imagined than this compellation. Eblis, according to Arabian mythology, had suffered a degradation from his primeval rank, and was consigned to these regions, for having refused to worship Adam, in obedience to the supreme command: alledging in justification of his refusal, that himself had been formed of etherial fire, whilst Adam was only a creature of clay. *Al Koran*, c. 55, &c.

115. *the fortress of Aherman.* In the mythology of the easterns, Aherman was accounted the Demon of Discord. The ancient Persian romances abound in descriptions of this fortress, in which the inferior demons assemble to receive the behests of their prince; and from whom they proceed to exercise their malice in every part of the world. *D'Herbelot*, p. 71.

116. *the halls of Argenk.* The halls of this mighty dive, who reigned in the mountains of Kaf, contained the statues of the seventy-two Solimans, and the portraits of the various creatures subject to them; not one of which bore the slightest similitude to man. Some had many heads; others, many arms; and some consisted of many bodies. Their heads were all very extraordinary, some resembling the elephant's, the buffalo's and the boar's; whilst others were still more monstrous. *D'Herbelot*, p. 820.

Some of the idols worshipped to this day in the Hindostan answer to this description.

Ariosto, who owes more to Arabian fable than his commentators have hitherto supposed, seems to have been no stranger to the halls of Argenk, when he described one of the fountains of Merlin:—

> Era una delle fonti di Merlino
>
> Delle quattro di Francia da lui fatte;
>
> D'intorno cinta di bel marmo fino,
>
> Lucido, e terso, e bianco più che latte.
>
> Quivi d' intaglio con lavor divino
>
> Avea Merlino immagini ritratte.
>
> Direste che spiravano, e se prive
>
> Non fossero ai voce, ch' eran vive.
>
> Quivi una Bestia uscir della foresta
>
> Parea di crudel vista, odiosa, e brutta,
>
> Che avea le orecchie d'asino, e la testa
>
> Di lupo, e i denti, e per gran fame asciutta;
>
> Branche avea di leon; l'altro, che resta,
>
> Tutto era volpe.

117. *holding his right hand motionless on his heart.* Sandys observes, that the application of the right hand to the heart is the customary mode of eastern salutation; but the perseverance of the votaries of Eblis in this attitude, was intended to express their devotion to him both heart and hand.

118. *In my life-time, I filled, &c.* This recital agrees perfectly with those in the Koran, and other Arabian legends.

119. *Carathis on the back of an afrit.* The expedition of the afrit in fetching Carathis, is characteristic of this order of dives. We read in the Koran that another of the fraternity offered to bring the Queen of Saba's throne to Solomon, before he could rise from his place, c. 27.

120. *Glanced off in a whirl that rendered her invisible.* It was extremely proper to punish Carathis by a rite, and one of the principal characteristics of that science in which she so much delighted, and which was the primary cause

of Vathek's perdition and of her own. The circle, the emblem of eternity, and the symbol of the sun, was held sacred in the most ancient ceremonies of incantations; and the whirling round deemed as a necessary operation in magical mysteries. Was not the name of the greatest enchantress in fabulous antiquity, Circe, derived from Κιρκος, a circle, on account of her magical revolutions and of the circular appearance and motion of the sun her father? The fairies and elves used to arrange themselves in a ring on the grass; and even the augur, in the liturgy of the Romans, whirled round, to encompass the four cardinal points of the world. It is remarkable, that a derivative of the Arabic word (which corresponds to the Hebrew רהס, and is interpreted *scindere secare se in orbem, inde notio circinandi, mox gyrandi et hinc à motu versatili, fascinavit, incantavit*) signifies, in the Koran, *the glimmering of twilight*; a sense deducible from the shapeless glimpses of objects, when hurried round with the velocity here described, and very applicable to the sudden disappearance of Carathis, who, like the stone in a sling, by the progressive and rapid increase of the circular motion, soon ceased to be perceptible. Nothing can impress a greater awe upon the mind than does this passage in the original.

121. *They at once lost the most precious gift of heaven—Hope.* It is a soothing reflection to the bulk of mankind, that the commonness of any blessing is the true test of its value. Hence, Hope is justly styled "the most precious of the gifts of heaven," because, as Thales long since observed—ὁις αλλο μηδεν, αυτη παρεστιν—it abides with those who are destitute of every other. Dante's inscription over the gate of hell was written in the same sense, and perhaps in allusion to the saying of the Grecian sage:—

> Per me si va nella città dolente:
>
> Per me si va nell' eterno dolore:
>
> Per me si va tra la perduta gente.
>
> Giustizia mosse 'l mio alto fattore:
>
> Fecemi la divina potestate,
>
> La somma sapienza, e 'l primo amore.
>
> Dinanzi a me non fur cose create,

Se non eterne, ed io eterno duro:

Lasciate ogni speranza, voi che 'ntrate.

canto iii.

Strongly impressed with this idea, and in order to complete his description of the infernal dungeon, Milton says,

——————where——————

——————————hope never comes

That comes to all.

Paradise L. 1. 66.

ABOUT THE AUTHOR

WILLIAM THOMAS BECKFORD (October 1760–May 1844) was born in London, England, to a wealthy, esteemed family. The only (legitimate) son of William Beckford (Alderman Beckford, who twice held the office of Lord Mayor of London), he inherited vast family wealth at the age of ten, when his father died unexpectedly. This inheritance was so prodigious, it made him one of the richest individuals in all of England, consisting of £1 million cash (over $150 million U.S. by today's standards), as well as immense English estate holdings and ownership of several sugar plantations in Jamaica. Young William went on to indulge in a life of extreme debauchery, whimsy, scandal, and artistic fulfillment.

As a child he received piano lessons from Wolfgang Mozart and throughout his life wrote copious amounts of music. He was also trained in art and architecture and became an eccentric collector and purveyor of art from around the world, often selling priceless collections, only to purchase them back years later when the mood struck. Most famous of these endeavors was his construction of Fonthill Abbey, a colossal "country house," said to be the most sensational building of the English Gothic Revival, built to house a library collection that he purchased.

In 1782, before his twenty-second birthday, Beckford travelled to Italy and penned his first book, *Dreams, Waking Thoughts and Incidents* (first published in 1783). Upon his return to England later that year, he wrote *Vathek*. Beckford claimed it only took him three days and two nights, but its polish suggests otherwise. The book was not published until 1786, when Rev. Samuel Henley translated the work into English and arranged for publication in England, without Beckford's name, as *An Arabian Tale, from an Unpublished Manuscript*, adding extensive notes. The first French edition (dated 1787) was published later in 1786.

After 1784, Beckford exiled his young wife and himself from England for about twelve years after he was publicly outed for a reputation of sexual aberrancy (bisexuality with a youth, as well as involvement in multiple other affairs); although he was never "officially" sentenced, his prestige was forever scarred. (Curiously, thirty years later, George Gordon, Lord Byron, who lived much the same sexual life as Beckford, also self-exiled to Switzerland but was lionized by the press and literati. Byron was reportedly inspired by *Vathek* to pen his epic poem *The Giaour.*) Beckford spent the time abroad travelling through much of Western Europe and publishing travel memoirs that were widely read (particularly *Letters from Italy with Sketches of Spain and Portugal*, 1835). He was an avid reader and involved in literary circles across the continent, including a particularly close friendship with author Jane Austen.

Though hardly destitute by the end of his life, Beckford had managed to lose most of his holdings and was valued at less than £80,000 (less than $1 million U.S. today) upon his death at the age of eighty-three, leaving behind two grown daughters (each married into nobility), and a legacy of artistic unconventionality and luxuriant patronage. *Vathek* slowly gained cult status and is recognized today as an important example of Gothic literature, influencing the poets and writers of nineteenth century Romanticism.

SUGGESTED DISCUSSION QUESTIONS FOR CLASSROOM USE

1. *Vathek* is a unique novel in that there is no hero or heroine. The protagonist caliph is villainous, as are the antagonists that counter him. Readers are at a loss for a likeable character to empathize with or to "root for." In what other ways does author William Beckford instead draw in the reader to keep them vested throughout this story?

2. Vathek's insatiability for knowledge drives the plot of this story. "*...for he wished to know everything; even sciences that did not exist.*" What does this mean to you? Can you imagine any sciences that do not exist, but perhaps someday could?

3. The closing decree against Vathek, Carathis, and Nouronihar, et. al. was that once their hearts took fire, they "...at once lost the most precious of the gifts of heaven—HOPE." Do you agree with this statement that hope is the most valued notion humans have? Or do you disagree? What else could be argued as more important than hope?

4. After telling in great and lengthy detail about the fall and ultimate punishment of Vathek and company, William Beckford ends the story with a singular line (almost as an afterthought) regarding Gulchenrouz—who played a relatively minor role in the story—indicating that he passed his life in "undisturbed tranquility, and the pure happiness of childhood." Why do you think the author ended the story in such a way?

5. *Vathek's* greatest success seems to have come by way of influencing other authors, including Lord Byron and John Keats in the nineteenth century, and H. P. Lovecraft and Clark Ashton Smith in the twentieth, who all cited the book as inspirational in its style and imaginative qualities. What elements in the book or the literary style of the author could you see as inspirational to yourself or to other authors?

6. The term of Orientalism is used today to define a method of viewing Arabic people and culture in distorted and "uncivilized" or harmful ways. Often this image has been employed to reflect Western culture (i.e., "us" being readers of English or other Latin-based language) as familiar and holding socially acceptable views, contrasted against Eastern or "Oriental" culture, which is portrayed as strange, irrational, and often barbaric. Do you think this novel succeeded (at least partly) because of its Oriental setting, which made for sensationalist reading in its time (the late eighteenth century)? Could this book have been just as successful if the

author had changed the setting and culture to any other land and people?

7. Genii (known also as djinn) are supernatural spirits who are portrayed throughout literature and movies in countless ways from benevolent guardians to demonic tricksters. In this book the antagonistic Genius is depicted by Giaour, who tempts and ultimately leads Vathek into Eblis's underground realm, along the way demanding fifty children to devour. However in the book there are also benevolent Genii, such as the one who rescues Gulchenrouz and bestows upon him perpetual childhood. Why is it important to show the differences of alignment within this mythical race?

8. A literary theme is a main idea that a story presents, whether directly (or repeatedly) as a "major theme" or indirectly (or briefly) as a "minor theme." *Vathek* has numerous literary themes such as pride precipitating a downfall, the inequity of social order, the role of motherhood, etc. What are some other themes you can identify within this book?

9. Consider the adage: "Absolute power corrupts absolutely." For Vathek, who possessed seemingly insatiable appetites along with unchecked power, the story's ending seemed somewhat preordained. In terms both of a cautionary tale and by the certainty that the magnitude of his mounting transgressions can only, eventually, overwhelm him, could this book have ended any other way than by retribution

against his atrocious deeds? If his power had been checked or weakened early on, could that have ultimately saved him?

10. *Vathek* is categorized as a Gothic novel, although it is set in Oriental culture rather than the customary backdrop of castle, graveyard, church, or other locale of medieval-inspired architecture. Rather the classification comes more from the induction of a sense of terror for the reader as well as the emphasis on the supernatural. What do you consider are some of the most memorable or noteworthy supernatural elements in this story? Do you think each was needed as part of the plot or were they merely to populate and accentuate a tale of mystical journey?

11. Vathek and company set out on a great journey, both literally and metaphorically, to discover the palace of subterranean fire (the domain of Eblis), where they expect to discover the secrets of the universe. How important to you is it to travel to new places and discover unfamiliar things? How far would you travel to obtain something you desire?

12. This book presents a view of religious "indifference," meaning Mahomet, as the Holy Prophet of Allah, witnesses Vathek's pride and excesses, but chooses not to intervene, stating to the Genii, "Let us leave him to himself... let us see to what lengths his folly and impiety will carry him." Do you think this is for the best, to let individuals make their own way without interference (or unasked advice) from others,

or should one with knowledge and means involve themselves in other people's lives, even if without invitation, if such act is reasoned to be charitable?

13. Vathek blames his mother for his final punishment: "...the principles by which Carathis perverted my youth have been the sole cause of my perdition!" To what degree is he right, that she has driven the course of his life to this inexorable conclusion? To what degree is he wrong, that Vathek is responsible for his own choices?

14. In a moment of magnanimity, a benevolent Genius, in the form of a shepherd, offers Vathek one last chance for redemption. Vathek nearly accepts it, until his pride rises up, and he sends the Genius off with scorning remarks. Looking back, Vathek might very well have regretted that decision. Have you ever done something you've later regretted? What lessons were you able to take away from the incident in order to make better choices the next time?

SUGGESTED FURTHER READING
OF FICTION

For readers who have enjoyed *Vathek* and wish to further read works of similar voice, theme, or literary style, consider the following, which represent just a small selection of available great and commensurable novels.

Arabian Nights and Days: A Novel (Arabic: *Layali alf lela*) by Naguib Mahfouz (1979): In this sequel and companion novel for *One Thousand and One Nights*, familiar characters continue their fantastic adventures.

The Black Spider (German: *Die Schwarze Spinne*) by Jeremias Gotthelf (1842): In this gothic horror tale, a woman makes a pact with the devil in order to save a town from the tyranny of their ruling feudal lord, only to learn a crueler fate when she tries to forego the devil his due.

The Blind Owl (Persian: *Boof-e koor*) by Sadegh Hedayat (1936): The narrator, a young and despairing opium-addicted painter, is driven to madness by nightmares while he obsesses over a beautiful woman.

Divine Comedy (Italian: *Divina Commedia*) by Dante Alighieri (3 parts: 1308–1320): Considered one of the greatest

works of world literature, this narrative poem is told in
three parts, detailing the author's journey through Hell,
Purgatory, and Paradise.

The Episodes of Vathek (French: *Vathek et les episodes*) by
William Beckford (1787): Written as a continuation of
Vathek, and told to the Vathek character by other "sinners"
awaiting judgement in Eblis, these episodes relate the
carnal and evil tales of their lives.

Faust (German: *Urfaust*) by Johann Wolfgang Von Goethe
(2 parts: 1772–1775): A retelling of the Faustian legend,
in which a doctor seeking knowledge of the divine trades
his soul to the devil; this version has an ultimately more
benevolent ending.

The Giaour by Lord Byron (1813): An epic poem, set as
an Oriental romance, revolves around three narrators
who each have a different point of view about a woman
belonging to a harem who is drowned for the offence of
adultery, and the revenge taken on her master by her lover,
the giaour.

Haroun and the Sea of Stories by Salman Rushdie (1991): A
young boy, Haroun, is son of a legendary storyteller, living
in a city so sad it has forgotten its own name. One day his
father's stories end, and Haroun sets out to restore the
tales.

Hasan by Piers Anthony (1969): In the days of Sinbad, an
adventurous young man is guided by Allah to travel the
Arabic landscape, and, in doing so, battles all manner of
monster and evil in order to learn his life's desire.

The History of Nourjahad by Frances Sheridan (1750): A Persian
youth is taught valuable lessons of character by his childhood
friend, sultan Schemzeddin, by being led to believe he has
become immortal and gained inexhaustible riches.

Melmoth the Wanderer by Charles Robert Maturin (1820): A
series of "tales nested within tales," in which a scholar sells his
soul to the devil in exchange for 150 extra years of life, then
searches the world for someone to take over the pact for him.

The Monk: A Romance by Matthew Gregory Lewis (1796):
A Spanish monk forgoes his monastic vows when giving
into temptation of increasingly depraved acts of sorcery,
murder, incest, and torture.

The Necromancer; or, The Tale of the Black Forest (German:
*Der Geisterbanner. Eine Wundergeschichte aus mündlichen
und schriftlichen Traditionen*) by Lawrence Flammenberg
(Karl Friedrich Kahlert) (1794): A gothic novel of
murder, ghosts, and dark magic, structured as a series
of interconnected stories, all centering on the enigmatic
figure of Volkert the Necromancer.

*Night & Horses & the Desert: An Anthology of Classical Arabic
Literature* (an anthology) edited by Robert Irwin (2002):
An anthology containing excerpts from numerous works of
classic Arabic literature, dating between fifth to sixteenth
centuries along with commentary explaining their
significance to the historic world as well as the modern.

One Thousand and One Nights (AKA *Arabian Nights*) (Arabic:
Alf Laylah wa-Laylah) by various authors (later including
Antoine Galland) (c. 800): Possibly the most famous
collection of Middle Eastern folk tales, including stories
originally penned in multiple languages by authors over
several centuries, along with favorite characters later added
by Antoine Galland such as Aladdin and Sinbad the Sailor.

Paradise Lost by John Milton (1667): An epic poem in ten
books concerning the biblical story of the fall of man
and the Angelic War over Heaven as told from multiple
perspectives.

Peter Schlemihl's Miraculous Story (German: *Peter Schlemihls wundersame Geschichte*) by Adelbert von Chamisso (1814): A novella in which a young man trades his shadow to the devil for a "bottomless wallet," only to later regret his decision and make atonement for the remainder of his life.

The Picture of Dorian Gray by Oscar Wilde (1890): A young man trades his soul for perpetual youth and beauty; his portrait ages instead of him, recording the years and his hedonistic sins.

The Rubáiyát of Omar Khayyám (Persian: trans. from various quatrains) by Omar Khayyám (c. 1120): A collection of Arabic poetry, written by various authors, though all ascribed to Khayyám, discussing such topics as beauty, myth, and creation.

The Shaving of Shagpat by George Meredith (1856): A humorous Oriental romance composed of stories within stories, in which a barber and enchantress go against a tyrant whose power is held in his magical hair.

The Tales of the Genii: or, the Delightful Lessons of Horam, The Son of Asmar by Sir Charles Morell (James Ridley) (1764): A collection of short fantasy tales modeled on those of *Arabian Nights*, originally published in two volumes.

Tales of the Marvellous and News of the Strange (Arabic: *al-hikayat al-'ajiba wa'l-akhbar al-ghariba*) by various authors (c. 800): Historically notable as the earliest known Arabic fantasy short stories, a third of which were expanded upon to include within the original *Arabian Nights*.

The Tragical History of the Life and Death of Doctor Faustus by Christopher Marlowe (approx. 1589): A dramatic Elizabethan tragedy in which the titular character makes pact with the devil, exchanging his soul for 24 years of knowledge and power to do as he likes.

Zofloya, or The Moor by Charlotte Dacre (1806): A
purposefully melodramatic gothic tale of scandal, sexual
deviancy, and violent revenge, in which a wicked heroine
shuns the mores of aristocratic views to reach her own
ends.

ABOUT THE SERIES EDITORS

Eric J. Guignard has twice won the Bram Stoker Award®, been a finalist for the International Thriller Writers Award, and been a multi-nominee of the Pushcart Prize for his works of dark and speculative fiction. He has over one hundred stories and non-fiction credits appearing in publications around the world, has edited multiple anthologies, and has created an ongoing series of primers exploring modern masters of literary short fiction, titled *Exploring Dark Short Fiction*. His latest books are his story collection, *That Which Grows Wild* (Cemetery Dance) and novel, *Doorways to the Deadeye* (JournalStone).

——

Leslie S. Klinger is the *New York Times*–bestselling editor of the Edgar®-winning *New Annotated Sherlock Holmes* and the Edgar®-winning *Classic American Crime Fiction of the 1920s*, as well as numerous other annotated books, anthologies, and articles on Holmes, Dracula, Lovecraft, Frankenstein, mysteries, horror, and the Victorian age. Twice nominated for the Bram Stoker Award® for Best Nonfiction, his work includes the acclaimed *New Annotated Dracula* and *New Annotated H. P. Lovecraft*, as well as the World Fantasy Award–nominated *New Annotated Frankenstein* and several anthologies of classic vampire and horror fiction. His latest books are *New Annotated H. P. Lovecraft: Beyond Arkham* and *Annotated American Gods* with Neil Gaiman.